John Henderson, John Ireland

Letters and Poems

John Henderson, John Ireland

Letters and Poems

ISBN/EAN: 9783744716260

Printed in Europe, USA, Canada, Australia, Japan

Cover: Foto ©Andreas Hilbeck / pixelio.de

More available books at **www.hansebooks.com**

LETTERS AND POEMS,

BY THE LATE

Mr. JOHN HENDERSON.

WITH

ANECDOTES OF HIS LIFE,

BY

JOHN IRELAND.

———— If a man do not erect in this age his own tomb 'ere he dies, he shall live no longer in monument than the bell rings, and the widow weeps.

SHAKSPEARE.

LONDON:

PRINTED FOR J. JOHNSON, NO. 72, ST. PAUL'S CHURCH-YARD.

M,DCC,LXXXVI.

P R E F A C E.

OUR Second Charles, of pleaſant and good-natured memory, obſerving Gregorio Leti, the Italian hiſtorian, attending his levee, aſked him how his book went on; for, ſaid the King, " I am informed you intend publiſhing Anecdotes of the En‑ gliſh Court.   Take care there be no offence in it."   " Sire," anſwered the Italian, " I am collecting materials for ſuch a work,

A 3

and

and will be careful as poſſible; but, unleſs
a man be wiſe as Solomon, he cannot
publiſh Anecdotes without giving ſome
offence." Why then, replied the Monarch
" cannot you be wiſe as Solomon? write
Proverbs and let *Anecdotes* alone."

The counſel was good, and counſel have
I alſo received.

I was told, he that wrote of thoſe who
were living, or *ſtept upon aſhes which were
not yet cold*, ought not to inſert his name in
the title page; for it was committing himſelf, and might create enemies. The advice
had influence, but not the influence which
was intended. Conſcious of meaning to

publiſh

publish truth, and truth only, I venture to prefix my name to this book.

The person of whom I write, had once my warmest partiality, and living with him in habits of the most unreserved intimacy, I knew him well. The motives which actuated his conduct, are explained in his letters; that I now possess them, and the fragments of poetry which he gave me, is owing, in some measure to accident, and, in some degree, to a habit I have of preserving any thing, however trifling, which is the production of a friend. On my once shewing a number of little sketches by the late Mr. Mortimer, a gentleman asked me, if I had hoarded up the cuttings of his pencils.

From

From Mr. Henderſon's letters, I have endeavoured to ſelect ſuch as tend to explain his theatrical ſtory, or ſuch as from their *naiveté*, pleaſantry, and good ſenſe, place his powers in a light, which, I think, gives them a diſtinguiſhed rank in that claſs of writing. It is ſcarce neceſſary to premiſe, that they were not intended for the preſs, and therefore exhibit, *not* the writer and his labours, but the *man* in his natural character.

I am apprehenſive it may be thought that ſome of them are unimportant, and relate to private tranſactions, with which the public have no concern, and that I might have compreſſed the volume, by omitting the introductions and concluſions of thoſe to my-

ſelf,

felf, which frequently contain merely a repetition of the fame profeffions of friendfhip,
only expreffed in different words; but I
think, that originality of turn which he frequently gives to the moft trifling circumftance, fuch a mark of his mind, as ought
not to be withheld by him who profeffes to
publifh his letters; and I am inclined to
look upon that editor who lops off, at his
own difcretion, any branches with which he
happens to be diffatisfied, as fometimes doing
more than his duty warrants.

There are fome mifcellaneous epiftles
written at a very early period of his life:
the few which I have inferted that were addreffed to him, need not any apology for
their publication.

The

PREFACE.

The poems which are subjoined, considered as hasty effusions rather than finished
compositions, as the productions of a
man who had received few aids from
education,* and whose only guides were a
classical taste, formed by having read, with

a power

* It is not intended to insinuate this as an apology.
I thought they had merit, or I would not have published
them. Nothing can be more contemptible than pester-
ing the public with reams of nonsense, by young gentlemen under fourteen years of age, black women, men-
mercers, ostlers who cannot spell; and esquires, who
can do little more.

If a work has merit enough for the public eye, that
public will generally protect and encourage it; and if it
has not, its being written while the author was standing
upon one leg, or standing upon his head; written with

his

a power of difcrimination, fome of the beft
Englifh writers, prove that he poffeffed imagination, and aptitude of poetical expreffion,
which might, had he made poefy the object
of his purfuit, have been cultivated into
excellence.

Attached to his previous reputation, they
may excite curiofity, and, I hope, gratify it,
by exhibiting his talents in a new point of
view.

The high eftimation in which his abilities
were held by men of diftinguifhed rank
in literature, the ample teftimony which

was

his fingers, or written with his toes; written in feven
days, or feven months, are very infufficient reafons to
give for its appearance, in an age when the prefs teems
with hourly births, of which we only know, that " *they
were born, and died.*"

was given to his merit as an actor, and the eminent honours which were paid to his memory as a man, first suggested the idea of publishing his letters and poems. I reviewed what had my early approbation, and time has not much sunk them in my opinion.

It has been suggested to me, that my notes are too numerous, and too long, but I could not well abridge, or incorporate them with the work. 'Tis the error of inexperience; for this is the first book I ever ventured before the awful tribunal of the public. If I have pardon from my readers, and should ever publish another, that fault shall be avoided.

ANECDOTES

A CLAIM of literary honours, for men who have not received a fcholaftic education, is, I am confcious, liable to be contefted.* The avenues to that portal of the Temple of fame, are guarded by the giants of learning, who, mounted upon pedeftals, compofed of huge tomes

B   of

---

* It feems a general axiom, that he who has never felt *birch*, fhould never wear *bays*.

of folios, quartos, and duodecimos, which only prove, *that men were dull in ancient days,* look down with sullen contempt on the adventurer who is hardy enough to attempt gaining access through any other than the prescribed and beaten path.

This temple, as was that of the Druids, is kept sacred from the intrusion of the un-hallowed multitude, and the unanealed man, who attempts to snatch a sprig of the holy missetoe, is in some danger of being sacri-ficed upon the altar, as a propitiatory offer-ing to the offended deity of the place.

Of those whose eminence hath been thought worthy of Biography, we frequently read, that they received the rudiments of their education from one learned man, and were assisted by the instructions of another,

then

obtain many advantages. He was indeed very ill ufed. Part of his employment was

was a " *cooking animal*†;" he dreſt and ſold alamode beef; and I am told, that the truffles and morrels which he uſed in making up this compoſition, led him to the ſtudy of natural hiſtory. At one period of his life he kept a chandler's ſhop, and could metamorphoſe a ſprat into an anchovy, ſubſtitute dried willow leaves for tea, and mix fine ſand with his Liſbon ſugar; he was a good carver, a tolerable button-maker, and, I was near ſaying, not a contemptible buffoon; but with the utmcit ſub-miſſion to thoſe ingenious gentlemen, who excel in imitating the noiſe a horſe makes when he is drinking, the purring of a cat, braying of an aſs, croaking of a raven, or lowing of a cow; ſuch qualifications would have entitled him to no higher a claſs than, *an imitating animal,*

† The beaſts, have memory, judgement, and all the faculties and paſſions of our mind, in a certain degree; but no beaſt is a cook.

BoswELL's Journal, p. 25.

was to drive his mafter in a one horfe chaife to fome academies where he taught, in the neighbourhood of London, and to feed and rub down the horfe, on his return to town.

During his ftay with Fournier he made a pen and ink drawing from a print of a fifherman fmoking his pipe, with fundry accompaniments

animal, rather more cunning than a monkey, and rather more active than an oyfter; but Fournier would bear the teft of Dr. Franklin's definition. He was a *tool-making animal*‡; he made gravers, and modelling inftruments.

When we confider the number of profeffions he attempted, can we wonder that he did not attain very great excellence in any?

‡ No animal but man makes a thing, by means of which he can make another thing.

Mr. JOHN HENDERSON.

——— QUÆ DOCTUS ROSCIUS EGIT.

HOR. EP. AD AUG. 82.

A CLAIM of literary honours, for men who have not received a fcho-laftic education, is, I am confcious, liable to be contefted.* The avenues to that portal of the Temple of Fame, are guarded by the giants of learning, who, mounted

B   upon

* It feems a general axiom, that he who has never felt *birch*, fhould never wear *bays*.

upon pedeſtals, compoſed of huge tomes of folios, quartos, and duodecimos, which only prove, *that men were dull in ancient days*, look down with ſullen contempt on the adventurer who is hardy enough to attempt gaining acceſs through any other than the preſcribed and beaten path.

This temple, as was that of the Druids, is kept ſacred from the intruſion of the un-hallowed multitude, and the unanealed man, who attempts to ſnatch a ſprig of the holy miſletoe, is in ſome danger of being ſacrificed upon the altar, as a propitiatory offering to the offended deity of the place.

Of thoſe whoſe eminence hath been thought worthy of Biography, we frequently read that they received the rudiments of their education from one learned man, and were aſſiſted by the inſtructions of another,

then

then configned to an univerfity, where they added to their claffic knowledge, and *rich in the ftores of ancient Greece and Rome* burft into fociety, where they were gazed at with the eye of expectation, and gratified with reiterated praife.

Indeed thefe gentlemen do not *always* give indications of having obtained many advantages by their ftudies, yet are they fpoken of, as men who from their education muft be in poffeffion of great powers, if they could but be prevailed upon to exert them.

Very different was the introduction of Mr. Henderfon; of Greek he was totally ignorant, and little acquainted with Latin.*

He

---

*. A fhort time before he went to Bath, a clergyman, by whofe partiality I am honoured, and who has kindly

permitted

He had no claim to hereditary honours, nor title to any paternal inheritance. ✝ He was the builder of his own fame, and the founder of his own fortune, for had not his talents brought him into celebrity, and given him the power of acquiring independence, it is not probable that any one would have enquired who was his grandfather.

permitted me to enhance the value of this volume by the publication of one of his letters, pointed out the courfe of his ftudies, and gave him fome affiftance in an attempt to attain that language; but Henderfon's mind was too volatile for the *gradus ad Parnaffum.*

✝ It has been faid he was defcended from Doctor Alexander Henderfon, of Fordyll; for this there is no authority, except the name being fpelt in the fame manner. He believed his family were originally Irifh, but whether they were or not, he neither knew nor cared. He thought, with Sir Thomas Overbury, that the man who has nothing to boaft of but his illuftrious anceftry, is fomewhat like a potatoe, the only good thing is under ground.

father. Of his grandfather, however, thofe who wifh it may read in the Memoirs of an unfortunate young Nobleman, by which Memoirs, and fome collateral evidence, it appears that he was a Quaker, and a warm adherent to the caufe of Mr. Annefley. That in conjunction with feveral others, he adventured a confiderable fum in fupport of the Anglefey lawfuit, which being loft, the money advanced was never recovered by himfelf or Henderfon's father, who was an Irifh factor in Goldfmith - ftreet, Cheapfide, where Mr. John Henderfon was born in February 1746-7.

By his father's death in 1748, his mother was left with a very flender pittance, and two fons totally dependent upon her. She retired to Newport Pagnell, where a clofe attention to œconomy enabled her to

fupport

ſupport herſelf and family upon the intereſt of leſs than a thouſand pounds. *

In this place, with no other tutor than his mother, Henderſon paſſed the early part of his life. She taught him to read, pointed out the proper authors, and induced him to imprint upon his memory, and recite, ſelect paſſages from Shakeſpeare, Pope, Addiſon, or any other Engliſh claſſic in her poſſeſſion.

The

---

* The eldeſt ſon ſhe apprenticed to a Mr. Clee, an ingenious engraver, in Oxendon-ſtreet, and the young man gave early promiſe of great profeſſional talents; but being of a very delicate habit, fell into a decline, and was removed to Paddington, where happening to lodge in the ſame houſe with the afterwards celebrated Kitty Fiſher, and being ſuddenly ſeized with a violent fit of coughing, the good-natured girl ran to his aſſiſtance, and he died in her arms.

The wonder-working magic of the old bard inchanted his imagination, * opened a new creation to his fancy, and prompted him to enquire how thofe characters were reprefented which afforded him fo much delight in the perufal. The defcription promoted a moft eager wifh to fee a play, a wifh which could not then be gratified, for in Newport-Pagnell there were no players.

Learning and reciting the fpeeches improved a memory naturally tenacious, and gave him an early relifh for polite literature.

By

* The firft play which attracted and delighted him, was, *The Winter's Tale,* and he often declared it was fortunate for him, the commentators had not been about his mother's edition. It was without notes ; which, faid he, confufe, perplex, and embarrafs me *now.* God help me, what would they have done *then ?* I fuppofe they would have crazed *me,* as they have other people.

By this was his tafte formed, and as the writer of thefe anecdotes has frequently heard him declare, by this he acquired what knowledge he had of the Englifh language, for of the rules of grammar he was totally ignorant. *

It would be defrauding his memory of a debt due from juftice, fhould I omit to remark that he not only always fpoke of his mother's attentions with filial gratitude, but when his fituation enabled him to follow the impulfe of his mind, made her happinefs his firft care.✝   She lived to fee her inftructions matured by time, and the

public

* I think it is faid, that Cowley's fchool-maſter could never prevail upon him to learn the rules of grammar; yet, from the profe-writings of Cowley, who that has read them will with-hold praife.

✝ This will appear by feveral letters in this volume.

public diftinguifh and protect what fhe had planted and foftered.

At about eleven years of age he went to a fchool at Hemel-Hemftead, taught by the late Doctor Stirling, where he did not remain above twelve months, but fhort as the period was, contrived to enlarge his acquaintance with the Englifh claffics, to acquire fome knowledge of French, and learn the common rules of Arithmetic.

From this place he returned to London, and having fhewn an early propenfity to drawing, was placed as a kind of houfe pupil to the late Mr. Fournier, who was then a Drawing-Mafter, a man poffeffed of great verfatility of talent, but deftitute of that prudence which might have rendered his abilities ufeful to himfelf or family.*

* Fournier's conduct, or rather want of conduct, feems to have been very fimilar to what the Duke of

Buckingham's

From a perfon of this defcription it is not to be fuppofed young Henderfon could obtain

Buckingham's would probably have been, had his Grace ranked with plebeians. Fournier was,

" In the courfe of one revolving moon,
" Engraver, painter, fidler, and buffoon."

His grand ambition was being able to do what any other man could, and having a happy facility, in the courfe of a few years he diftinguifhed himfelf as an en-graver, painter, mufician, carver, modeller in wax, and teacher of drawing and perfpective, with which he was fo well acquainted as to compofe a book on the fubject, upon the principle of Doctor Brooke Taylor, which has confiderable merit. In the firft edition, is an etching from an early defign of Mr. Gainfborough's, which Henderfon told me was etched by himfelf, without any affiftance from his mafter.

If we try Fournier by Mr. Bofwell's definition of man, he will be found to have had fome merit. He

was

obtain many advantages. He was indeed very ill ufed. Part of his employment

was

was a " *cooking animal†*;" he dreft and fold alamode beef; and I am told, that the truffles and morrels which he ufed in making up this compofition, led him to the ftudy of natural hiftory. At one period of his life he kept a chandler's fhop, and could metamorphofe a fprat into an anchovy, fubftitute dried willow leaves for tea, and mix fine fand with his Lifbon fugar; he was a good carver, a tolerable button-maker, and, I was near faying, not a contemptible buffoon; but with the utmoft fub-miffion to thofe ingenious gentlemen, who excel in imitating the noife a horfe makes when he is drinking, the purring of a cat, braying of an afs, croaking of a raven, or lowing of a cow, fuch qualifications would have entitled him to no higher a clafs than, *an imitating animal*, rather more cunning than a monkey, and rather more active than an oyfter; but Fournier would bear

the

---

† The beafts, have memory, judgement, and all the faculties and paffions of our mind, in a certain degree; but no beaft is a cook. BOSWELL's JOURNAL, p. 25.

was to drive his mafter in a one horfe chaife to fome academies where he taught, in the neighbourhood of London, and to feed and rub down the horfe on his return to town.

During his ftay with Fournier he made a pen and ink drawing from a print of a fifherman fmoking his pipe, with fundry accompaniments

the teft of Dr. Franklin's definition. He was a *tool-making animal*‡; he made gravers, and modelling inftruments.

When we confider the number of profeffions he attempted, can we wonder that he did not attain very great excellence in any ?

Ars longæ, vitæ brevis eft.

‡ No animal but man makes a thing, by means of which he can make another thing.

accompaniments in the ſtile of Teniers. This, as the production of a boy under fourteen years of age, obtained him the honour of the ſecond premium from the ſociety for the encouragement of arts, and the ſtile in which it was executed ſhews an accuracy of eye, and power of imitation, very rarely the lot of one ſo young.

As this boyiſh production was higher in my eſtimation than his own, in the infancy of our friendſhip he gave it me, but as it was the only ſpecimen of his drawing, I preſented it to Mrs. Henderſon on her marriage, and am informed it is now in the collection of Sir John Elliot.

Soon after this time he came to live with Mr. Cripps, a working ſilverſmith in St. James's-ſtreet, to whom his mother was related, and her intention was that he

ſhould

fhould learn that trade, but the death of Mr. Cripps put an end to this fcheme, and he was left at about twenty years of age with very few connections, and without any determinate purfuit.

His only refource feemed to be that of becoming an affiftant in a filverfmith's fhop, but even this fituation, humble as it may feem, was not very eafy to obtain ; for, on application to a perfon of the trade, the higheft terms offered were twenty-five pounds a year. A propofal was foon after made him to become out-door clerk to a banker, upon a falary little better than the foregoing. Both thefe offers he communicated to a friend, who warmly oppofed his accepting terms fo very inferior to what his abilities ought to command, and advifed him to turn his attention to the ftage, for which he thought him eminently qualified; but Hen-

derfon

derfon hefitated at this advice, declaring his circumftance did not enable him to wait the tedious delays of managers. Being, however, affured, that he might confider the houfe, intereft, and purfe of his friend, at his fervice, until he was fituated to his own fatisfaction, he directed his endeavours to an introduction amongft the *Dramatis Perfonæ*; endeavours in which he encountered difficulties, delays, and mortifications, which cannot be conceived by thofe who have not been in fimilar fituations; which would have abated the vigour of purfuit, and cooled the ardour of expectation in almoft any other man; but he feems to have poffeffed, even at that time, a confcioufnefs of talents that when feen, would force themfelves into notice, and when noticed muft be encouraged.

He

He however paſſed his time eaſily and chearfully, in the ſociety of a family where he was treated with all the attention that friendſhip could prompt, by whom his intereſt was conſidered as connected with their own, who ſincerely eſteemed him, were pleaſed with his talents, and gratified by his pleaſantry; and perhaps it would not have been eaſy to point out a man who poſſeſſed ſuch convivial powers as he did in the younger part of his life. His obſervation was quick, his comprehenſion ample, his manners moſt lively and conciliating; but the ludicrous light in which he ſaw and frequently exhibited any object that preſented itſelf, created him enemies, who, though they were pleaſed with his wit had no great reliſh for his ſatire, when exerciſed upon themſelves*.

* A city dealer in little trinkets, whoſe ever ſmiling face bears ſome reſemblance to Lord Monboddo's

Aborigine,

The Ode to the memory of Shakefpeare being at this time popular, Henderfon at-

tempted

Aborigine, became ambitious of being enrolled an artift in an exhibition catalogue, made a copy of the Duke of Leinfter's arms in *human hair*, and brought it for Mr. Henderfon's approbation, telling him he wifhed a *pat* infcription written under, that it might be noticed in the exhibition room. " Sir, (fays Henderfon) I will give you one, that had you known and confidered the advice of the Delphic oracle, you would have chofen for yourfelf : it fhall be allufive." " Thank you, Sir," fays the other.—" You obferve, (continued Henderfon) the fupporters are two monkies rampant, proper, and very pretty they are indeed ; lend me a pen, Sir, and I will write you an infcription from the great Milton. Here it is : read it aloud, Sir."

————— " *In their looks divine,*
" *The image of their glorious Maker fhone.*"

Happening to fee a manufcript, which one of his friends was preparing for the prefs, entitled, " Original

C

Tales

tempted it in Mr. Garrick's manner, and with such success, that it must have been a very accurate ear which could distinguish one speaker from the other*.

Some of the consequences which resulted from this talent, he describes in the following letter to a young divine:

Tales for the Instruction of Young Gentlemen and Ladies," he inscribed in the title page the following quotation :

"T A L E S !

" *Told by an ideot, full of sound and fury,*
" *Signifying nothing.*"

The book was not published.

* His first public exhibition was in a barn, or some such place, at the polite village of Islington, where he recited the Ode for the benefit of a few unfortunates, who called themselves a company of comedians.

One of the audience, who had retired from the plains of Devonshire to breathe the pure air of Islington, in his

later

To the Reverend Mr. P——.

I Find T—— has written to you.   I ſuppoſe you will correſpond with him.   He ſent me his farce with a meſſage, begging me to offer it to Dibden, which I have declined, as thinking it more properer to preſent it either to Garrick or Colman.   I wiſh it may anſwer his expectations.   Does not a wiſh ſometimes imply a doubt.——
* * * * * * and I ſat in judgement upon it the other night, and brought in our verdict—*Ignoramus.*

I am glad you told me of the thirty manuſcript ſermons, I ſhould elſe have roſe

C 2

early,

later years, declared he was certain, the ſpeaker *muſt be*, either Mr. Garrick, or Antichriſt.

early, and late took reſt, to tranſlate Flechier's and Bourdalon's for you. L——
thinks you are dead; for aſking me how you
did, I replied, you ſlept with your fathers, I
made him happy by telling him it was a me-
taphorical ſleep, and that you would awake
a profound theologiſt.

It was a very raſh propoſal I made to you
of commenting upon authors. I thought it
might have been done, but when I go about
it I feel myſelf ſtrangely confined in my
powers, like thoſe who do not apprehend the
danger of a precipice till they are on the
brink. I think I will give up the thought
'till you are more at leiſure. R—— I ſeldom ſee. L—— never. Thoſe hours
I am not with I—— are paſſed in
drinking, and writing ſerious reflections on,
and bitter invectives againſt, drunkenneſs,
both in verſe and proſe. If this contra-

riety

riety continues, and heaven only knows how long it may continue, you may expect a satire against fornication written from Marjoram's.——Is not this in your language the character of one *buffeted by Satan?* B——, in the simplicity of his heart told me, one day, after much bewailing the reduction of his circumstances, " that it was a great mercy he had not *taken* to drinking," feeling himself, I suppose, totally unable to resist any impulse which it should please Lucifer to embarrass him with. I saw your letter to E——, wherein I stand recorded as a fool for quoting Macbeth upon such a subject as your laziness—and this is owing to my modesty, that would rather talk in other people's words than my own. But

" Hence ye vain fears of criticism, hence,
By caution nurs'd, at happiness' expence;

To

> To prove my pen in trite quotations run,
> Thine own the quibble, and thine own the pun;
> Take thine full fwing, and in the critic's fpite,
> If nonfenfe urge thee, freely nonfenfe write."

I will make you repent the reproof, for talk I muft—and if it is all my own. But you have brought it upon yourfelf, and fo are lefs to be pitied. E—— writes with me. His will be a good letter, and I am glad I have found the way of diverting your indignation. He will put you into fpirits, and you will read mine with better temper.

I wifh we could form a triumvirate at T——'s; he has written me a very genteel and preffing invitation. I have traces upon my memory of much happinefs with him, and it was a happinefs that I like, independent of auxiliary hogfheads. There is a natural feftivity in him that will always

entertain,

entertain, and I have known him ſtart much excellent wit and good-natured ſatire. I believe matrimony draws off a man's genius; his letters to me are not near ſo pleaſant, nor ſo brilliant as they were wont to be. I ſuppoſe you will rebuke me for that me-taphor, and therefore you may eraſe *genius, and inſert attention*, which is the ſame thing with thoſe like you, with whom deſire is power.

There is a burleſque parody of Garrick's Ode publiſhed, on Le Stue, cook to the Duke of Newcaſtle, and teſtimonies to his genius and merit prefixed.

I wiſh Garrick's had been ſtill at the bot-tom of Avon, from whence I am ſure he fiſhed up ſome of it; for it has ruined my conſtitution in ſpeaking it. I have been up till three in the morning, four nights a

week,

week, for this month paſt. Inſtead of
ſleep, I get flattery; and inſtead of dream-
ing of Miſs ————, claret.

I wiſh I could convey to you a few ſounds
which the boobies about me ſay are exceedingly like Garrick's, but they would have no
melody mixed with the poſtman's horn. If
I could get a cake of Rabelais' ice, in which
to mix them, they would thaw by your
veſtry fire, and give you ſome idea of London flummery. But our air is not intenſe
enough to make ſuch a cake; therefore you
muſt take it on my word, that I am flattered, inebriated, ſpoiled—Yet, as a *bon
vivant* I owe it ſomething, for it has
brought me acquainted with diſhes I never before heard off—wines I never before
taſted—and fruit I never before ſaw, except through the fruiterer's windows.—
I eat pine-apple the other day, and if

that

that be the fruit the Devil offered Eve, I
don't fee how fhe could refift it.——Otway
has dealt a little unfair in his bitter in-
vective againft women————

" And for an apple damn'd mankind."

He fhould have added that it was a pine-
apple; with all my dramatick faith, I never could believe it was worth her while
to tranfgrefs for a mere apple, even though
it had been a nonpareil.

S H A N D Y.

At

At this time he belonged to an evening fociety, confifting of about twelve or
fourteen members, who wifhed to unite
to the feftivity of Anacreon, the humour
of Prior, the harmony of Pope; and, above
all, the fenfibility and pleafantry of
Sterne*.

Part of the plan of this club, who met at
a houfe in Maiden-lane once a week, was,
to fubftitute fome toaft, in the place of a
health to the political idol of the day, or the
premier of the month, about whofe real
principles their different partizans are fometimes a little in the dark, and whofe very
names are the roots from whence fpring up
difputes,

    " About it, goddefs, and about it."

that

---

* The name they adopted was the Shandean fociety.

that do not much tend to inform, or en-
liven the unfortunate hearers, and frequently
end in

" Contention fierce, endlefs debate, and hate irrecon-
cileable."

To avoid which evils, it was a rule, that
when the fociety meet, the Prefident pour
a libation, and drink to the memory of fome
departed genius, with whofe merits every
perfon prefent either was, or might be
acquainted, under the denomination of a
SKULL; after which, the next man gave
a *fentiment*, and the next a *fkull*. If for
inftance, they had drank the memory of
Shakefpeare, it was expected that he who
was next in progreffion, fhould give a fentiment, which fhould have fome allufion to
the bard, or his writings, *and be new*. One
equally appofite, was, to follow the names

of

of Rabelais, Cervantes, or Sterne. But, alas! it was soon found that such a rapid succession of skulls to sentiments, and sentiments to skulls, promoted so quick a circulation of the glass, as to clash with part of the plan of the institution, which was to go home tolerably sober*.

To correct this inconvenience, it was ordained in council, that each member should bring with him a volume of his favourite writer, and read such part aloud as he thought would most contribute to the amusement of the society. Henderson produced a volume of Sterne, the god of his idolatry,

entered

---

* It was observed by a theatrical veteran, who sometimes honoured this society with a visit, that " though it was a very pleasant and chearful thing to get drunk, it was a very disagreeable busines to get sober."

entered fo fully into the fpirit of his author, fo happily difcriminated the characters, and fo forcibly exhibited them, that his companions finding more gratification in hearing him than themfelves, which I believe will be acknowledged as ftrong a teftimony of approbation as could be given by a fociety compofed of reading men, conftituted him reader to the club, and without an act of parliament, confirmed his right to a name which had been given him by a friend a fhort time before; decreeing that from, and after that time, he fhould be diftinguifhed by the name of SHANDY, an appellation he retained many years.

The manner in which he read Sterne's works, threw new light upon many paf-

fages,

fages†, and was the fource of much information as well as pleafantry. In the
humorous paffages it called forth flafhes of
merriment, and drew tears from every eye
in the pathetic. Never fhall I forget the
effect he gave to the ftory of Le Fevre. It
kindled a flame of admiration, and promoted a propofal to devote a day to the
memory of the author, pour a libation over
his grave, and fpeak a requiem to his departed fpirit*.

This

† It was firft obferved in this fociety, that until the
appearance of the four afterifks (* * * *) with which
Sterne has fo frequently embellifhed his volumes, the
two following lines were totally mifconceived:

———— " If weak women go aftray,
" Their *ftars* are more in fault than they."

* A rainy day prevented the full completion of the

plan.

This was the determination of a moment, and aſſented to with enthuſiaſtic eagerneſs. Shandy was appointed to ſelect what he thought moſt fit for the occaſion, and the next week produced an Ode, on which the candid critic will look with ſome allowance, when he conſiders it as the haſty production of a man little more than twenty years of age. The ardour with which the ſubject is treated, will, I hope, be conſidered as an adequate apology for the inaccuracies in ſome of the lines.

The occaſion of its being written, the idolatry with which the name of Sterne was venerated by the company who attended the recital, and, above all, the energy, and pathetic

plan. The Ode was, therefore, read to a ſelect party in a private houſe.

thetic feeling which was diſplayed by the ſpeaker, gave it a moſt powerful effect, and it has ſurely too much merit to be buried in oblivion.

O D E.

O D E.

INTENDED TO HAVE BEEN SPOKEN AT THE TOMB

OF THE LATE LAWRENCE STERNE,

ON HIS BIRTH DAY.

T H I S day be facred,—let no hoftile found,
Prophane the honours deftin'd to his fhade,
Hence ye unhallow'd from this votive ground,
No gueft improper on our rites pervade.
Before his name let wanton fatire fly,
The ftoic's rancour melt before his beams,
Let fpleen avoid the lightning of his eye,
And fink for fhelter in oblivion's ftreams.
Hence too, unfeeling and cold blooded gueft,
Dull ignorance, in folemn garments dreft.

But come thou Goddefs fair and free,
On earth y'clep'd Philanthropy,
Fill our bofoms, crown our board
With all thy fpirit can afford.
Thy fon, thy elder born we fing,
Sound the hautboys, tune the ftring,

D

Need'ft

Need'ft thou, goddefs, need'ft thou learn,
All our notes are rais'd to Sterne.
To him our grateful notes afcend,
Him we folicit to attend.

If 'midft the fpheres,
Tun'd by the bright angelic choir,
Thy fpirit hears
The tribute of a mortal lyre,
Deign, oh deign to fhed thy power,
Thy mighty magic on this feftive hour.
Nor, when my grateful verfe reveals,
What every fon of candour feels,
Let thy gentle foul difdain,
What alive had given thee pain ;
Our motives thou may'ft try above,
And know our praife the tribute of our love.

Shame to the man, and to his memory fhame,
Whofe tongue licentious robs thee of thy fame.
Oh hadft thou liv'd when critics learn'd and wife,
To juftice faithful, own'd no other ties ;
Dupes to no party, and no flaves to fear,
In fentence candid, yet in judgment clear,

Feeling

Feeling like men, like men their sentence own'd
Nor honour'd dullness, though by dunces thron'd,
Then had thy sacred bust in triumph rose,
And twining laurel screen'd thee from thy foes.
But he unhappy fell on evil days,
When *barren* sentiment usurp'd his praise.
When folly bore the honours and the crown,
Which should have deck'd his temples with renown.
When he from virtue greatest honour drew,
And held philanthropy to public view,
Adorn'd with all that can secure esteem,
The monarch's glory, and the poet's theme,
That balm of blood and confidence of mind,
Impell'd to pity, to suspicion blind,
That bosom, open to each social claim,
In virtue ardent, negligent of fame;
That heart, unable to repel relief,
In courage manly, feminine in grief.
In pleasure, harmless, innocent, and mild,
Warm as a man, forgiving as a child,
Ev'n then they dar'd to violate his page;
In virtue barren, fruitful in their rage,
Vex'd, inly vex'd, that on inspection clear,
They search'd their hearts and found no Toby there.

D 2   Stung

Stung, inly ſtung, they ſnatch'd the pen,
And told the taſtelefs ſons of men,
That he whoſe ſpirits warm and full,
Could charm the gay, and wake the dull,
Could fix a ſmile on ſorrow's brow,
And ſteal his grief he knew not how.
Could give new courage to the brave,
And bid his fame ſurvive the grave,
Could give religion freſher charms,
And lead the ſtoic to her arms,
Could bid, (on touching fancy's ſtring,)
Profuſion in a defart ſpring,
Benign vibrations ſtir the trees,
And chearful rapture ſwell the breeze,
That he, with all theſe powers fraught,
Was looſe in language, and impure in thought;
Believing virtue, their 'monition took,
And thank'd his ſtars he had not read the book.

    The idle crew,
    Who never knew
More than theſe mighty critics choſe,
    Soon caught the ſound,
    And echoed round,
The friends of Sterne were virtue's foes;

                              Error

Error confirm'd, what malice had begun,
Till fool and critic, loft their name in one.

Some there arofe who fpurn'd the flavifh tie,
And if they cenfur'd, would at leaft know why;
But all too indolent, or all too dull,
His fruits to gather, or his flowers to cull,
    The loofer parts
      Attach'd their hearts,
But when they hop'd fome grofs defect to clafp,
His wit, like Mercury, efcap'd their grafp.

If high in blood, voluptuous in thought,
Some beam of beauty's emanative fire,
As fwift the meteor glided by he caught,
    It play'd perhaps around his heart,
    But urg'd not foul defire.
    Some kindred tendernefs it warm'd,
    Which ftraight to other themes he drew,
    No longer virtue ftood alarm'd,
But join'd his paffage as he upward flew.
Too weak of wing, or impotent of fight,
Thefe readers loft him in the daring flight:
Thus envy ftung, or dullnefs veil'd his worth,
·*Till nature, warm and zealous in his caufe,

D 3   Snatch'd

Snatch'd him at once from this ill-judging earth,

To realms where angels hail'd him with applause.

Cervantes gaily grave, with accent sweet,

And laughing Rabelais led him to his seat;

Yorick, in flashes of wild transport roar'd,

As when in Denmark's court he shook the board.

The social shades of tenderness and love,

Spread the glad tidings through the courts above.

    All heard, all flew on wings of joy,

    And welcom'd him to peace sincere,

    To bliss whose raptures never cloy,

    And happiness unknown to fear.

To us belongs to vindicate his fame,

To pluck the nettle from his sacred grave,

To turn the darts of malice from their aim,

And point his virtues to the good and brave;

Nor this a task which indolence would shun,

'Tis half-accomplish'd when 'tis once begun;

Obvious and full they strike upon the sight,

Nor ask assistance from collected light,

Oh!

Oh ! when ye hear his memory defam'd,
His wit misconstrued, or his heart bely'd,
Loud be his warm benevolence proclaim'd,
'Till rage and error blushing turn aside.
Whate'er their motive, ignorance, or whim,
They slander'd nature when they slander'd him.

For me, I own, with grateful transport mov'd,
I love his memory, as the man I lov'd.
Dear to my eye, but dearer to my heart,
Ne'er felt my soul more agonizing smart,
Than when that spirit from its bondage fled,
And gave a second Yorick to the dead.

Besides

Befides Sterne's works, he fometimes read felect paffages from Milton, Pope, Prior, Swift, Gray, and Junius.

The verfification of Pope was too fmooth for him, the fame found fo perpetually recurring upon the fame fyllable, gave a flatnefs which fatigued the ear. The meafure became vapid and lifelefs. From this cenfure I except his manner of reading the Dunciad, to which he gave the full force of its fatire.

Gray's Elegy he always miftook; by endeavouring to exprefs energy, he deftroyed that plaintive folemnity which is furely its peculiar characteriftic. Indeed, the fpecies of poetry in which this Elegy claims the firft place, did not feem to be his *forte*. If he attempted the pathetic it became a whine, and his ear being too correct to

bear

bear the founds of his own voice, he changed his tones, and quitted his author's manner, preferring impropriety to diffonance. In the light airy tales of Prior, where laughing whimficallity is the predominant feature, he was on his proper ground. To " the manly vigour of one fterling line " of Churchill, he added a thoufand beauties. Junius, he efteemed the moft perfect model of Englifh profe, and although unacquainted with the politics of the day, gave full effect to every fentence of that moft fplendid writer. Paradife Loft he deemed a dramatic poem; ftrongly varied the different manners of Moloch, Belial, and the other fallen angels, and entering with fublime energy into the fpirit of the various characters, became, as was faid of his author, as a chariot-wheel wrought into a blaze by its own motion. It was grand, forcible, terrific.

But

But his talents as a reader are so well known from the specimens he exhibited at Freemasons-Hall, that it becomes unnecessary to expatiate upon them here. I am not afraid to aver, and it is an opinion grounded upon some reflection, that he read better in Maiden-lane than he did in Queen-street: it was less theatrical, and more chaste.

It is not very usual for the Dramatis Personæ to distinguish between acting, reciting, and reading; when reading they attempt to act, and imitate the passions which they are only required to enumerate.

In reading a letter to an audience, they do not always think it necessary to change their intonation. It is *acted*, and uttered with all the buskined pomp of heroic emphasis. Of this error Henderson was never guilty.

Mr.

Mr. Garrick was, I believe, efteemed to have approached very near perfection in playing, that he was above mediocrity in reciting or reading, no man will, I think, affert, who has heard him read, or recite his Jubilee Ode.

The great requifites neceffary to conftitute a reader, feem to be, a good ear, a voice capable of inflexion, an underftanding of, and tafte for, the beauties of the author, and a feeling, an ardour, an enthufiafm, which will warm the mind to difplay them; to all this muft be added a judgment that will guard againft extremes. Whether Mr. Henderfon was, or was not, in poffeffion of *all* thefe requifites, is a queftion I will not prefume to decide. I think he read better than any man I ever heard.

He

He ufed to fport an opinion, that the great difference of reading confifted in under-ftanding, or not underftanding, the author's meaning. I mentioned inftances where men had written with great knowledge of their fubject, and expreffed their fentiments in glowing and brilliant colours, who yet fo totally mangled and weakened their own works when they attempted to read them, as to obfcure the brighteft paffages, and dif-guife the moft obvious fentences. " Sir, faid he, reft affured, they did not fully under-ftand what they read. Some men have a trick of ftringing words together, fo as to impofe upon the underftanding, but they do not wholly conceive what they are about. Let any one be fully and powerfully im-preffed with an author's meaning, and if his voice and articulation are not defective, he cannot fail impreffing that meaning upon his hearers. A female mendicant under-

ftands

ſtands what ſhe wants, and therefore her entreaties are uttered in the tones beſt calculated to reach the heart, and with an emphaſis that rarely offends the ear. A thoroughly enraged ſcold is infinitely more pointed in her oratory, than is a gentleman in a wig and band at Weſtminſter-hall.

" She is animated from conceiving her ſubjeƈt, and feeling the paſſion, ſhe repreſents it. An infant is perfeƈt maſter of the art of ſupplication before he can ſpeak, and when he attains that power never aſks for any thing with an improper emphaſis until he is *taught* to read, when he is harraſſed about points, confounded by a multitude of inſtruƈtions, and ſent to a *Demoſthenes maker*, who gives him rules for utterance, and modes of ſpeech, and a *manner* of delivery, that enables the well inſtruƈted young gentleman

man to torture the ears of all within compafs of his voice, whether he is doomed
to exhibit in the pulpit, or the fenate, at
the bar, or upon the ftage. The human
voice is in a great degree artificial, and
whatever any one chufes to make it. You
find general fimilarity in the tones of people of one profeffion. One fet of tones
are appropriated to the bar, another to
the pulpit. I have heard that moft fublime compofition, the burial fervice, flo-
vened over in fuch a manner that I could
fcarcely underftand two words in a fentence,
and yet the voice has had a kind of folemn found, a pious noife, that has given
great effect.

" Sounds have infinite power without words.
This fhould feem to extend to mufic, but
with me it does not. I have little gratification from what I am told is exquifite.

Some

Some one fays, it is become the art of exe-cuting difficulties. It was a good wifh, would to heaven thefe *difficulties* were *im-poffibilities*.

" When I recited Mr. Garrick's Ode in a private room, I felt what I faid, and I believe gave it fome effect. Very diffe-rent was it upon the ftage. My feelings were weakened and confounded by the band, my voice loft its fcale, and was overpower-ed by the mufic in the orcheftra."

This, it muft be acknowledged is a rhapfody, and as fuch was fpoken, but there are fome truths in it.

Mr. Pope exhibited an inftance, that a man may have the moft delicate ear for the harmony of numbers, and yet have no fort of tafte for the harmony of founds.

Swift

Swift is another example, and I am inclined to fufpect from Mr. Garrick's manner of finging, that he had not, whatever he might chufe to profefs, much knowledge of, or tafte in, mufic.

Would it be fuppofed from the meafured, harmony of Dr. Johnfon's periods, that he had fcarcely any perception of it. He knew a drum from a trumpet, and a bagpipe from a guittar, which he owned was about the extent of his knowledge in mufic*.

Mr. Henderfon had great delight in perufing books that abounded in the marvellous. Sir John Mandeville's Travels, Pontoppidan's Norway, Peter Wilkins' Voyage to the Moon, or Wanley's Wonders of the

Little

* Bofwell's Journal, 1ft edition, page 363.

Little World were *in deliciis*.* With equal
eagernefs he fought for and read the ac-
counts

* We fay *Nofcitur a Socio*—May we not, with equal
truth, fay, *Nofcitur a Libris*.

A knowledge of the particular fpecies of books which
attract men of genius and ftudy in their hours of de-
fultory reading, would be curious and worth fpeculation :
fuch knowledge might fometimes enable us to develope
the bias of their characters with more truth than do
their graveft biographers.

For the gratification of the curious I have fubjoined
the titles of a few books in Mr. Henderfon's ftudy, in
fome of which the ludicrous and the horrible, " for
mafterfhippe do ftrive."—The lamentable and true Tragedie of Maifter Arden of Feverfham, who was mofte
wickedlie murdered by means of his wantonne Wife,
who hired two defperate Ruffians, Blacke Will and
Shakbagge, to kill him. Life and Death of Lewis
Gaufredy, with his abominable Sorceries, after felling
himfelf to the Devil. A bloody Newe Yeares Gifte. A

E

true

counts of murders, battles, maffacres, mar-
tyrdoms, earthquakes, the death of Regulus,

true Declaration of the cruel and moft bloody Murther
of Maifter Robert Heath, in his own houfe at High
Holborne, being the figne of the Fire Brande. A true
Relation how a Woman at Atherbury having ufed divers
horrid Imprecations, was fuddainlie burned to Afhes,
there being no Fire neare her. Hellifh Murder com-
mitted by a French Midwife. Hiftories of Apparitions,
Spirits, Vifions, and other wonderful Illufions of the
Devil. The Surey Demoniac, or Satan, his dreadful
Judgements upon Richard Dugdale. A Pleafaunte
Treatife of Witches, their Impes and Meetings. Newes
from Italie, or a moft lamentable Tragedie lately be-
fallen. *Phylomithie,* wherein outlandifh Birds, Beafts,
and Fifhes, are taught to fpeak Englifh. Tarquatus
Vandermer, his feven Yeares Studie in the Arte offe
Magicke upon the twelve Monthes of the Yeare. The
Devil Conjured, by Thomas Lodge : a Difcourfe of
the fottille Practifes of Divelles by Witches. The
Miferies of inforft Marriage. Lavaterus of Ghoftes
and Spirits walking by Night, and of ftraunge Noyfes,
Crackes,

gulus*, or burning of Cranmer, particulars of
a criminal's behaviour when broken upon the
wheel,

Crackes, *and fo forthe.* Baylie, his Wall Flower, as
it grew out of the ftone Chamber in Newgate. Ad-
mirable Hiftorie of a Magician, who feduced a pious
Womanne to be a Witch. And though laft, not leaft
in Love, King James, his Dæmonologiæ.

* A writer of the laft century has thrown this lamentable ftory into a moft ludicrous point of view. I
believe the lines are not generally known : perhaps it
will be faid they are not worth knowing ; however here
they are :—

When the bold Carthaginian,
Fought with Rome for dominion,
  Little Reg was ta'en in the ftrife ;
When his eye-lids they par'd,
Good Lord how he ftar'd,
  And could not go fleep for his life.

When

wheel, the barbarities Cortes and other zealous propagators of the gofpel inflicted upon the Indians, the tortures fuffered by the victims of fuperftition in the Inquifition, or any event whether in, or out of nature, which was calculated to give ftrong and forcible impreffions.*

By

When the bold Carthaginian,
Fought with Rome for dominion,
    Little Reg was ta'en in the quarrel,
So they took him up a hill,
And fore againft his will,
    They trundled him down in a barrel.

To thofe idolaters of ancient patriotifm, and ancient hiftory, to whom this defcription may appear a fhocking infult on the memory of fo celebrated a hero, it may be a confolation to recollect, that the beft critics and commentators, have efteemed the whole ftory of the death of Regulus, to be a fiction.

* If it fhould be inferred from hence that his difpofition was cruel, the inference would be unjuft.

Mortimer,

By the perufal of fuch books as thefe, objects of terror became familiar to his mind,

Mortimer, the hiftorical painter, in whom were united the favage grandeur of Salvator Rofa, and the terrific graces of Spagnolette; who, joined to a fublimity of idea, and accuracy of delineation, not exceeded by Michael Angelo, a delicacy of pencil equal to Teniers; was moft happy, and, I think moft fuccefsful, when fketching, or painting objects, from which the common eye withdrew. His four paintings of the progrefs of vice, in the very well chofen collection of Doctor Bates, of Miffenden, is one example of this truth.

From hints in Fox's Book of Martyrs, he made a number of moft fpirited fketches, in which are reprefented the fufferings of men, women, and children. Scorching their hands with lighted tapers, burning their eyes out with hot irons, and the whole exhibition of the ufes made of thofe powerful engines of argument, the whips, hooks, racks; but, above all, the *thumb vice*, by which unbelievers are fcrewed up to the proper faith.

E 3

Yet,

mind, and perhaps enabled him to exhibit with such warmth of colouring, portraits

Yet, with this disposition for contemplating, and displaying such objects, Mortimer had a soul, " Open as day to melting charity, a tear for pity," and a heart the most susceptible of tender impressions. He made the kindest allowances for the errors of others, and would not have trod upon the poor beetle. When he erred, and who shall dare to name any man as faultless? his errors had their root in virtues which the generous warmth of his heart carried to excess. Added to all this, he had an hilarity that brightened every eye, and gladdened every heart. I knew his mind well, but that knowledge should have deterred me from attempting to describe it, had I considered that Sterne has so exactly delineated the leading features by which it was actuated, in the benevolence and sensibility of character which distinguished his uncle Toby.

In the society of Mortimer I passed some of the happiest years of my life, and the remembrance of the very intimate, brotherly, and unbroken friendship with which

we

traïts of Shakefpeare's moft terrific characters, from which fpirits of a more
exquifite texture, unaccuftomed to the
contemplation of fuch objects, would
fhrink with horror. For I believe thofe
who have hearts of fuch fufceptibility as
to receive impreffions of joy, love, or
grief, in an extreme degree, are by no
means the moft eminently qualified for
communicating thofe impreffions to an
audience. A man whofe feelings are fo
alive as to overbalance the difproportionate
ftrength of his mind, becomes liable to
be awed into forgetfulnefs, the paffions are
overwhelmed in a ftorm of their own

E 4

raifing,

we were united until his death, affords me one of thofe
melancholy pleafures which may be felt, but cannot be
defcribed—A tear drops at the recollection. The lofs
of fuch a friend leaves a chafm in one's life and happinefs, which is very, very, rarely filled up.

raifing, and the actor drowned in a deluge of his own tears. The mind wrought up to real tendernefs, lofes, in fome meafure, the power of expreffing that which is fic-titious, and excefs of fenfibility defeats its own purpofe. * There is a point to which the paffions muft be raifed, to difplay that exhibition of them which fcatters conta-gious

* This may be thought at firft fight to clafh with the maxim of Horace; but, maturely confidered, may per-haps be found nearly to coincide with it.

I am told this is not the philofophy of the green-room, notwithftanding which, I fufpect the contrary opinion to be the philofophy of the diftaff. To fay, though with the utmoft dramatic dignity of emphafis,

" *He, muft, have, feeling, who, makes, others, feel;*"

May be replied to by,

" *Who drives fat oxen, fhould himfelf be fat.*"

gious tendernefs through the whole Theatre, but carried, " though but the breadth of a hair," beyond that point, the picture becomes an overcharged carricature, as likely to create laughter, as diffufe diftrefs. There is a certain *term* in the mind which is exactly proportionate to produce fympathy, *beyond* which limit, or *within* it, the effect ceafes to be produced. *

The

---

* It is a general opinion, that a good player muft have a found judgment, and conceive his author's meaning before he can exprefs it ; yet I have feen inftances where nature having denied an underftanding, has kindly given what did well enough as a fubftitute, and paffed mufter before an audience very dècently. Thefe inftances, indeed, were many years ago—I believe ;—but, inftead of an opinion, I venture an anecdote, and let the gentle reader draw his own conclufion.

When

The power of mimickry which Henderson poffeffed in a moft eminent degree,
and

.When the late Mr. Reddifh's indifpofition of mind
rendered him incapable of fulfilling his duties at the
Theatre, and he was by his inability reduced from a falary of twelve or fourteen pounds a week, to an income
of feventy pounds a year from the fund, fome of his
friends made intereft with the manager to grant him
a benefit. The play advertifed was Cymbeline, and
Mr. Reddifh was announced for Pofthumus. He
was to pafs an hour previous to his performance at a
houfe where I was afked to meet him. He came into
the foom with the ftep of an ideot, his eye wandering
and his whole countenance vacant. I congratulated
him on his being enough recovered to perform. Yes,
fir, replied he, I fhall perform, and in the garden fcene
I fhall aftonifh you !—In the garden fcene, Mr. Reddifh ?——I thought you were to play Pofthumus.—
No, fir, I play Romeo.—My good man, faid the gentleman of the houfe, you play Pofthumus. Do I, replied he ; I am forry for it. However what muft be,
muft be. At the time appointed he fet out for the
Theatre,

and exercifed with that indifcriminate negligent fportivenefs, which meaning no

evil,

Theatre. The gentleman who went with him, for he
was not capable of walking without a guide, told me
that his mind was fo impreft with the character of Romeo, he was reciting it all the way, and when he came
into the green-room it was with extreme difficulty they
could perfuade him he was to play any other part.
That when the time came for his appearance, they
pufhed him on the ftage, fearing he would begin
with a fpeech of Romeo. With the fame expectation
I ftood in the pit clofe to the orcheftra, and being fo
near had a perfect view of his face. The inftant he
came in fight of the audience his recollection feemed
to return, his countenance refumed meaning, his eye
appeared lighted up, he made the bow of modeft refpect, and went through the fcene much better than
I had ever before feen him. On his return to the
green-room, the image of Romeo returned to his mind,
nor did he lofe it until his fecond appearance, when the
moment he had the *cue*, he went through the fcene, and
in this weak and *imbecile* ftate of his underftanding,

performed

evil, feared no confequences, was the fource of fome inconveniences, which led him to repent having difplayed it in the unguarded manner he frequently did.

Mr.

performed the whole better than I ever faw him before, and it was a character in which I had feen him often, and never contemptible. But he appeared to much greater advantage then, than when he had the full exercife of his reafon. His manner was lefs affuming, and more natural. After that time he never performed.

It brought to my recollection an anecdote I have heard of his late majefty, who, naming an officer that he intended fhould command in an expedition of fome confequence, was told by the Duke of Newcaftle that " the gentleman was by no means eligible for fo important a ftation, being pofitively mad." Is he, replied the king, he fhall go for all that, and before he fets out I wifh to my God he would bite fome of my Generals, and make them mad too."

Mr. Garrick, was at this time the object of his imitation, and not much gratified with the freedom, nor much difposed to ferve the perfon who took it; under thefe circumftances an introduction to him was difficult, his different friends were therefore fought out and applied to for their intereft. Among other applications, one was made to the late Paul Hiffernan, of dull memory, who was at that time one of the attendants at the managers *levee*.

When the name and intention of Henderfon was announced to Hiffernan, he looked in his face with the utmoft gravity for half a minute, and then, like a drill ferjeant giving the word of command, vociferated " *Pleafe to ftand upon your pins.*" — Henderfon ftood up. — Mr. Hiffernan did the fame.—— Now, fays he, young
gentleman,

gentleman, I'll foon fee if you'll ever make an actor.—I'll foon fee whether or not you are fit for the ftage. Then ftalking with folemn dignity to a table drawer, he opened it, and took out a ball of packthread, from which he firft cut off a long piece and tied the knife to the end, by way of plummet, this done marched up to the young candidate, and having firft got upon a chair, to be the better able to reach, held the packthread to the top of Henderfon's head, and let the knife drop to the ground, by which it was now feen he intended to try how tall he was. This ceremony over he defcended, took out of his pocket a two foot rule, and meafured the length of the packthread; then putting on a moft melancholy countenance, fhook his head, and exclaimed, " young gentleman, I am forry to mortify you, I am very forry to mortify you,

but

but go your ways home, fet your thoughts
upon fomewhat elfe, mind your bufinefs,
be it what it will, and remember I tell
you, for the fock or bufkin you won't do;
—you will not do, fir, by an inch and a
quarter.

This muft be acknowledged to be fomewhat in the fpirit of Serjeant Kite, but
it was Paul's mode of meafuring the talents of thofe who afpired to the ftage.
—*Excellent critic !*"

A theatrical veteran, whofe abilities have
been looked up to by the laft age with
admiration, and are regarded by the prefent age with aftonifhment; whofe judgment was thought matured by time, and
whofe decrees were uttered with that firmnefs and oracular dignity, which confounds
if it does not convince, and filences where

it

it cannot confute, was requefted to hear
Mr. Henderfon rehearfe, point out his
errors, and advife the beft method of improving his recitation. " Sir," fays this
Ariftarchus of the drama, " Sir, the young
man has genius, but the firft thing he
does muft be to *un*learn all that he has already *learned*, until he does that, he cannot
learn to be a player."

So fevere was the fentence of this Neftor
of the green-room, but even this, did not
deter the ftage-ftruck hero from his theatrical purfuit, he had the true enthufia-
ftic ardour which gains ftrength from op-
pofition; every difcouragement feemed rather to encreafe than abate his eagernefs;
and as accefs was not to be had to Mr.
Garrick, he endeavoured to obtain an introduction to fome of the other managers.
But managers, like minifters of ftate, were

not,

not, he found, very willing to hear, and when they did hear, not very eafy to pleafe.

One objected to him, that never having been upon any ftage, he was unftudied in his parts. Another excellent judge of the Englifh language, that in reading Pope, he made *verfe* of it. A third, that his voice was not ftrong enough for the ftage. A fourth, that his fpeaking was hufky, and his tones too fat.*

F He,

* His continual imitation of Mr. Garrick's voice, might, in a degree, contribute to give his own a refemblance of it; and that imitation was formed upon tones, which, melodious as they had once been, began to contract the hufkinefs fo commonly attendant upon old age. His fo frequently repeating fpeeches in the manner of Falftaff, gave what the fame critic calls a fatnefs of tone.

He, however, had friends, who renewed application to Mr. Garrick, and the manager's good underſtanding ſeemed to have vanquiſhed his reſentment, for he heard him rehearſe, ſaid, that his voice had neither ſtrength nor modulation enough for the London ſtage, but adviſed him to try his powers at a country theatre, for the purpoſe of forwarding an introduction to which, he would write to Mr. Palmer, then manager of the Bath company, who gave for anſwer, that he ſhould have an engagement, if approved of by Mr. Keaſeberry, who was then director of a *corps dramatique* at Richmond. Mr. Keaſeberry heard and approved, and, in September, 1772, Mr. John Henderſon was enrolled as one of the Bath comedians for three years.

The firſt year he was to receive one guinea per week; the ſecond, one guinea

and

and a half; and the third year, two guineas. Besides this enormous falary, he was to have an annual benefit.

The object of his ambition attained, he trembled with apprehenfion, doubted if his figure was fufficiently important, queftioned if he was grounded enough in any one character to venture it before the awful tribunal of the public, and could he have protracted his *entrée* for another year, would moft gladly have done it : fo great was his dread of difappointment and difgrace, that he affumed the name of Courtenay, and, under the protection of that name, made his *coup d'effai* at Bath, on the 6th of October, 1772, in the part of *Hamlet*.

The writer of this went with a number of friends from London to Bath, to fee the *debut'* of this young candidate for the dra-

matic

matic laurel, whofe apprehenfions were fo
alive, and whofe fears were fo exceffive, that
it was with difficulty he advanced upon the
ftage, and made his firft bow to the audience. They received him with that indulgence which is fo generally exercifed to a
young performer, and when he fpoke, gave
that ftill refpectful attention, which is perhaps a ftronger teftimony of approbation
than the thundering clapping of a thoufand
hands. But of the gratification which re-
fults from this mode of applaufe, he had a
large portion at the end of each act; and
before the conclufion of the firft, his fears
were fo far difpelled, and his terror fo much
fubfided, that his underftanding recovered
its natural expanfion; and although his
powers had not attained their full maturity,
yet the ftrong traits of judgment he difplayed in conceiving the outline of the part,
the fenfibility and feeling he exhibited

through

through the whole of the performance, the accuracy of his articulation, and the proper modulation of his tones, marked themſelves as diſtinctly as they did at any ſubſequent period.

In that fiery ordeal for dramatic candidates, Hamlet's advice to the players, he manifeſted ſo clear a conception of his author, with ſo much eaſe and propriety of recitation, as diſplayed his power of diſcrimination, and gave every right to augur the excellence he afterwards attained.*

Old

* When the performance ended, I went into the green-room—Let the reader of extreme delicacy avoid this note; or, if ſhe reads it, not accuſe me of omitting the proper warning.

Mr.

Old Mr. Giffard, under whoſe management,
Garrick made his firſt appearance, and
who had been witneſs to the dramatic riſe

of

Mr. Henderſon's predeceſſor, in the character, was
Lee, who uſed to play it in a ſuit of black velvet, much
too large for Henderſon ; he was, therefore, under the
neceſſity of performing it in a ſuit of black cloth. Extreme agitation occaſioned a perſpiration. The coat
was wet as if it had been " immerſed in the ocean."
The performance ended, Hamlet reſigned his habit to
the keeper of the wardrobe, who received it with aſto-
niſhment and horror ; hung it to the fire, lifted up both
his hands, and exclaimed, in the true naſal tone of a
pariſh clerk, " Heaven bleſs us all ! what a ſorry ſight
is here : 'twas the Lord's mercy he did not play it in the
black velvet——it would have raiſed all the pile. They
may talk of Muſter Lee, and Muſter Lee, and Muſter
Lee, but Muſter Lee is nothing to this man—for what they
call perſpiration." A perſon preſent obſerved, that the
ſevereſt critics muſt acknowledge the young gentleman
had played the character with great warmth, if not
with ſpirit.

of many of the moſt diſtinguiſhed actors. Who, in the courſe of a long life, had ſeen the dawnings and progreſſive exertions, of numbers whoſe abilities had been ſanctioned by public approbation; Mr. Giffard thought his talents of the firſt magnitude, deſired to be gratified by a morning's rehearſal upon the ſtage, when, with the ſpirit of prophecy, the old man foretold the future eminence of the young actor, returned to Ealing, and died in a few days.

Mr. Henderſon performed Hamlet a ſecond time a few nights afterwards; his feelings are deſcribed by his own words, in a letter which he wrote to a lady in London, and his reception, in ſome which he wrote to a clergyman, with whom he correſponded in the neighbourhood of London.

To

To Mrs. I———,

Bath, October 24th, 1772.

I AM obliged to you beyond my powers of expreſſion, for your kind ſolicitudes on my account. I haſte to anſwer them.—— I had a very full houſe to the ſecond Hamlet, and I played it much better than when you ſaw me, when my terror ſunk my figure and impaired my animation.—— I had a better audience ſtill laſt Tueſday to Richard, which (although I was more frightened then ever) I was much ap-plauded for.

I am a great favorite here, if being fol-lowed at the Theatre, and invited to pri-

vate

vate parties among people of confequence, are proofs of it.—I never took any thing kinder in my life than your coming to fee me; it was a mark of attention, friend-fhip, and regard, that, as I am confcious of not altogether deferving, delighted me exceedingly—It would have delighted me ftill more to have deferved it. But that you know is my fault—It fhall be cor-rected. You will find me very different in my manners.

Will you give my kind fervices to Mifs ——, though fhe is a forry jade and don't deferve them, for fhe has the info-lence to let my letter remain unanfwered. Yet, upon recollection, there may be kind-nefs in it, fhe may not be willing to engage me in a correfpondence to which I am un-equal. Adieu, my dear madam.—This is a

villainous

villainous fhort letter, but I muft break it off,

" Left Benedict fhould enter full of fear."

J. COURTENAY.

To the Rev. Mr. D——

Bath, 9th October, 1772.

DEAR DOCTOR,

YOU are among thofe of my friends whom I cannot fuffer to be unaddrefs'd by this opportunity of Mr. I——'s return. He will tell you my fuccefs, and you will feel that pleafure from it, which a mind and friendfhip like yours, cannot but feel, from the applaufe and approbation conferred on all you efteem and patronize.— I know, my dear fir, that I am very near

your

your heart, and I thank you, I efteem you, I love you for it. You diftinguifhed me when none elfe would; you encouraged me when others bore hard upon me. Never, never can I forget the kindnefs of your conduct towards me——Something too much of this. You muft excufe the fhortnefs of this letter, I have many to write, and very little time——Will you honour me with a line?——I cannot fay that I will anfwer it, but I will reply to it,——You will remember that my ftage name is Courtenay; to you, my dear fir, I will never fign any other than the name you gave me. I value it on that account, and therefore fubfcribe myfelf,

S H A N D Y.

To

To Mr. HENDERSON.

25th November, 1772.

DEAR SHANDY,

I cannot well defcribe the pleafure I received from the news of your fuccefs, without fome danger of expreffing myfelf in terms which, by the invidious, might perhaps be conftrued into flattery. This is one reafon why I have not anfwered your letter before, and not preffed forward among the firft lift of your congratulators.

Your letter, as it feems to have been dic-tated by a generous heart, which accepted the will for the deed, does you more honour than all your talents, brilliant as they are, and would to heaven my power had

been

been equal to my inclination, to render you any effential fervices. All friends here join in the general joy at the favourable account of Mr. Courtenay's reception.

As you know my real opinion of your genius and abilities, and that I never had any doubt concerning your fuccefs, provided your voice would hold 'out, it would be ridiculous to take up your time in paying compliments to that merit which I hope will foon be as confpicuous to the world, as it long ago was to me.

I truft you will not think the fhort advice which I am about to give, to be altogether impertinent; although your prudence and good fenfe may render it unneceffary.

Beware then, my dear friend, of the intoxication of applaufe, and remember that

great

great application, perseverance, caution, and continual efforts to improve, are principal, if not the only steps which can support you in your ascent to the summit of a lasting fame.

I hope you will avoid every species of intemperance, particularly that of the tongue. Do not despise the old adage, however trite it may be: viz. " Many a man hath sacrificed his friend for his joke." Be the player, but be the player no where but upon the stage. Out of the verge of the theatre, low buffoonery from a comedian, I hold to be errant prostitution. Why should not he be as much the gentleman as a person of any other profession ?

I mean not to lay any restraint, Shandy, upon the genuine sallies of innocent humour and wit, but upon that kind of pleasantry

and

and ridicule, the object of which is the de-
gradation of character : a vein of mirth
which fpecioufly pretends to exhilarate the
fpirits, whilft it infidioufly wounds the
heart.

Are you not ready, by this time, to break
out, and to exclaim in the language of rage
and impatience, " Something too much of
this preaching, my dear Doctor—you do not
confider that my ears are now open to no
founds but the thunders of an applauding
audience, and my eyes accuftomed to read
nothing with pleafure, or with patience,
but the *billet doux* of fome love-fick lan-
guifhing nymph."

May you, my dear Shandy, in your
public performances, be always received
with the heart-chearing plaudits of the judicious,

dicious, nor ever by your private conduct
forfeit the esteem and approbation of the vir-
tuous and good.

I am, &c.

To the Rev. Mr. D————.

Bath, Dec. 25, 1772.

My very Dear Doctor,

IT is so common a thing to fill letters
with excuses for their shortness, and apolo-
gies for want of time, that I am almost
ashamed of doing it, and yet the true reason
I have not replied to your friendly letter, is,
the intense fatigue of my studies, together
with the visits I am obliged to make; for
I find it necessary to be as attentive to my
reputation out of the theatre as in it; and

don't

don't think me vain, if I fay, that the more my acquaintance is extended, the more my reputation is encreafed——Enquire of me, Doctor, I am confident you can hear nothing of me which can difgrace your virtues to be in friendfhip with, or your genius to have diftinguifhed. I am in intimacy with a great many people of the firft rank and genius in Bath, and my connections are too polite to admit of the low buffoonery you caution me againft. I am now fituated to my heart's wifh, I converfe with men of letters, and am well received by them; I am in high favour with the manager, for which fee my letter to J. I——, a few days ago.

I have refumed my own name in a Prologue, written for me by a gentleman of great talents, and a painter, though not a painter by profeffion. His genius is like

G

the

the Dryades and Hamadryades, embofomed
in woods and fields. In plain Englifh, he
is, perhaps, the greateft landfcape painter
we have :

" By heaven, and not a mafter taught."

I muft tell you fomething which I know
will pleafe you. I am perfectly altered in
my manners. I can now be gay and merry
without being very licentious. I am willing to owe this to your advice, becaufe you
are among the few from whom it is not very
painful to receive obligations.

I have been on the ftage three months,
and I have played ten different characters,
all of the firft importance; this will fhew
you how I pafs my time, and convince you that it is not poffible for me to
have many leifure hours. Mr. Garrick has

done

done me great ſervices by writing of me to ſeveral of his friends here. I intend to write very ſoon to thank him for them—I thank Apollyon for his remembrance; make mine to him, and to all your family.

I am, &c.

J. HENDERSON.

To the Rev. Mr. D———.

DEAR DOCTOR,

I Wifh to reply to your laft friendly letter, but I have little or nothing to fay, and fcarce any time to fay that little or nothing in. It is needlefs to take up much time or paper, in affuring you, that I have a very great, and almoft filial affection for you; for I might fay that in three words, and tell you, I am grateful.

. I have played Lear with very great appro-bation, which I know will pleafe you, and I continue to be received with refpect, and

even

even friendſhip, almoſt wherever I go. You
may be aſſured I will forget none of your
excellent monitions to preſerve this, and indeed I am ſo far altered that I ſeldom jeſt,
and ſtill ſeldomer ridicule. I have every
reaſon to be ſatisfied with having come here,
for I could not have been more happy, I
think, any where, and I do not doubt
but that it will be for my future advantage.

The manager, I believe, eſteems me, for
no man can be more diſtinguiſhed than I am
by him. * * * * * * * * * *
* * * * * * * * * * * *.

I am extremely obliged to you for your
offer as to the *Claſſicks*, and I hope to ſhew
you in the ſummer, that I wiſh to improve

G 3

by

by your inftructions. You muft have patience, if I fometimes difcover too much
mifcellaneous rambling. I will be as attentive as I can.

I am, &c.

J. HENDERSON.

In

In the courfe of this feafon, the manager finding his new performer attracted
the attention of the public, introduced him
in near twenty different characters, to many
of which he muft have been very unequal. *

He however became popular, was fpoken
of by the title of the Bath Rofcius, in
high eftimation with the frequenters of
the Theatre, and diftinguifhed by the
friendfhip and protection of men, whofe
approbation will always confer honour and

G 4

create

* I have not a recollection of them all, but the principal were Hamlet, Richard the Third, Benedict, Macbeth,
Bobadil, which he attempted, and very fuccefsfully
performed, in the manner of Mr. Woodward ; Bayes,
Don Felix, Earl of Effex, Hotfpur Fribble Lear,
Haftings, Alonzo, and Alzuma ; he alfo recited Garrick's Ode.

create envy,* and in confequence of this was moft unmercifully abufed in the Bath papers both for what he did, and what he did

* Lord Newnham, whofe tafte is not lefs diftinguifhed than his rank.—Mr. Gainfborough, whofe portraits exhibit, not merely the map of the countenance, but the character, the foul of the original.—His landfcapes, —But to name works which fafcinate and delight every eye, is to praife. Mr. Philip Thicknefle, whofe partiality is the more valuable, as it is neither lightly or indifcrimi-nately beftowed. Of his warm regards, and friendly zeal, Mr. Henderfon, as well as the writer of thefe anecdotes, received many proofs. Mr. Taylor, very properly dif-tinguifhed, as the painter " by heaven, and not a mafter " taught;" and though laft mentioned, ever firft in kind and attentive fervices, the author of the Weft In-dian.

The

did not do * How far their satires gave uneasiness to the object they were aimed

at,

* The following little Epigram was written, I believe, by a gentleman of Bath, who afterwards became a partial friend to Henderson, and who is a proof that good sense and candour is open to conviction, for he acknowledged that his sentence was too harsh.

EXTEMPORE,

On Mr. COURTENAY's attempting to recite Mr. Garrick's Jubilee Ode, on the 9th of Dec. 1772.

When Courtenay spouted Garrick's Ode,
How did the man mistake his road;
And void of all the rules of art,
Distracted rave through every part,
Tearing his lungs, 'till out of breath,
Wild as the witches in Macbeth,
Whilst the old Bard who stood behind,
Attentive on his arm reclin'd,

Affected

at, will appear by an extract from a letter, dated 24th May 1773.

Affected at the murther'd tale
Trembled, and as his ghost look'd pale.

I thought the cloud-capt towers, and all
The gorgeous palaces would fall
With Shakespeare off his pedestal,
For the whole fabric tottering shook
From its foundations when he spoke ;
Garrick himself, had he been by
Had died————but not in extacy.

To

To Mr. J————.

———————— There is a writer here
" who has difcovered no talent, (but judgment in his fignature) called the INVALID,
who has, I hear, abufed me and my Prologue, * which has faved me a few fhil-
lings, for I was about to hire fomebody to
satirize

* A Prologue he fpoke 22d December, 1772, upon re-
fuming his own name, which follows:

(Written by JOHN TAYLOR, Efq. of the Circus.)

WHEN firft the advent'rous bard ftands forth to
view,
Thofe early fketches which with care he drew ;
When he, poor man, in lines uncouth and lame,
Juft ventures out a candidate for fame,

Trembling

satirize me into public conversation; the people here having agreed to applaud me

without

Trembling, he dreads a *damned* poet's fate,
The judges shrug—the carping critics hate.
Some partial friend, just at this anxious hour,
With chearing gaiety's reviving power,
Laughs at his doubts——" Nay, prithee don't recede,
Take courage man!—My word for't you'll succeed;
Out with your works, and let the world decide
On their true merit—while your name you hide."
This fancy strikes his weak distracted brain,
He smiles, and simpering, says, he'll write again.
Aye——but have patience, Tom, his friend replies;
The world—the world, my lad, has piercing eyes;
Mankind first try—by them alone be chear'd,
Their praise be courted, or their censure fear'd.
——The piece comes out by Tom, John, Dick, or
      Harry,
No matter which—perhaps it may miscarry.
But no—the learn'd approve and praise the style,
The ladies read it—e'en the critics smile.

Straight

without much enquiry why or wherefore.

Mr.

Straight to his friend he runs, to tell the news.
The world, dear fir, my work with pleafure views;
The firft edition, fir, I juft now hear,
Is quite run off———a fecond will appear,
And fince that met the applaufe I wifh'd to feel,
May I not now my real name reveal?

Ye candid fair, while wav'ring here I ftand,
In fad fufpence—O lend a helping hand;
May I, protected by your foftering care,
When critics murmur, to your court repair;
I have, alas! on this wide fea of fame,
Launch'd my poor bark, under a feigned name,
That if your frowns foretold a boifterous gale,
I might in time have lower'd my fhiv'ring fail; *
Have foon retreated from the ftormy main,
And hopelefs fhrunk into my port again.

May

* Shivering, a fea term when a fail is not wholly filled with the wind,
nor quite aback, as the feamen fay.

Mr. Colman has done me some service
of that sort, for which I always bow very
low to him, and he takes it for respect.*

The

May your kind favour still to me be shewn;
My merit pleads not—make the act your own;
And since you've deign'd to approve my weak essays,
From princely Hamlet, down to puzzling Bayes,
I now, with trembling hand the mask resign,
And hence appear before this beauteous shrine.

——————Courtenay no more!
O name so flattering to my fame-sick heart,
I bid farewell—we now, though friends, must part.
To thee thy borrower grateful tribute pays,
With thee, he hopes, not now to lose your praise.
Shine still propitious!—Still your smiles renew,
And Courtenay's pains in Henderson review;
Perfect the work that's now but rudely form'd,
And save the fruit, which in the bud you warm'd.

* Mr. Colman said, when Henderson performed
Shylock, his dress was so shabby it seemed just borrowed

from

The tide of partiality being high in his favour, he had in contemplation the purchafe of a fourth fhare in the Briftol Theatre. The money was provided, when he declined embarking in the fcheme, for reafons which appear in the following letter.

To

from a pawn-broker, and gave him the idea of a black Lear."

This cenfure falls with more weight upon the manager of the wardrobe, than the performer, and bears more refemblance to the cavil of a French taylor, than the candid critique one would have expected from the author of the Jealous Wife.

To Mr. I———.

Sunday Night, Nov. 1, 1772.

DEAR FRIEND,

THIS is the information I have gathered. The moſt money that has been
paid for any ſhare has been four hundred
pounds. There are four partners at 400l.
each, and one of them (the not acting manager) has forty pounds a ſeaſon allowed
him for his intereſt of the 400l. together
with the freedom of the Theatre for himſelf,
family, and friends. Three hundred pounds
a ſeaſon is paid for the rent, and the fifty
proprietors are admitted gratis to all performances whatſoever at the Theatre, which
is thought much overloaded. It was rather
a loſing ſcheme to Powell and Holland. It

is

is known that Mr. King loft above eighty pounds the feafon he held it; and the laft feafon, 'tis faid, each partner loft between one and two hundred pounds.

The whole property belonging to the partners, of clothes, fcenes, &c. is fuppofed to be worth under a thoufand pounds, and there are only two years to come of the leafe. There are three votes of the three acting managers in the conduct of the theatre.

There is no patent, which fubjects the managers to this inconvenience, that as their performers are not engaged by forms of law, they can quit them when they pleafe.

Thefe are the informations I have collected. It really does not ftrike me as any thing fo devoutly to be wifhed for. I can never ceafe to love you, my dear friend, for

the

the extreme folicitude you exprefs on this account. I really feel your zeal to ferve me, will, from its precipitance, go too far. I am myfelf utterly unqualified to manage players, and I muft be at the difcretion of

* * * * * * * * * * *.

Do, pray Jack, weigh it well. I have thefe informations from an authority you could not doubt, if I were at liberty to mention it—I am perfuaded, that if I chufe to play in the fummer at Briftol, I may make almoft my own terms, and then I have nothing to lofe.

It will be a great charge upon my mind, and I have need of all the time, attention and ftudy, I can have, to preferve the re-putation I have got here. Another thing is, I fhall want fome recefs from the fa-tigues of the feafon, and my chief hope and

ambition

ambition is, to pafs the fummer with you, and my other friends.

There may be foon a time when your kindnefs may find a more ferviceable exer-cife, and I am affured from your extreme goodnefs in this, that it will not lofe any of its ardour. You will obferve, that four hundred pounds is the moft that ever was given for any fhare, *and he afks* 400l.

I am of a patient, philofophical temper, and can live as well upon the little pittance I have as if it was larger, at leaft 'till my acquaintance is fuch as will require an ad-ditional expence in clothes.

In three words, I have not fet my heart upon it; on the contrary, if it is fecured for me, I fhall enter upon it with trepi-dation and doubt. I know L——— grounds

H 2

his

his opinion of its ſucceſs, upon the favourable reception I have met with here. But the people of Briſtol, I ſuppoſe, are like other people, capricious, inconſtant.

The theatre was ſupported, it ſeems, by them for one ſeaſon, but after that it flagged even when *Powell* was there.

Adieu, the bell rings.

J. COURTENAY.

When the Bath theatre clofed, he returned to London, and in his hours of unguarded pleafantry, frequently gratified himfelf and friends by ludicrous imitations of
the different performers, particularly Mr.
Garrick, who being informed that Henderfon's voice was fuch an echo of the green-
room, invited him to a breakfaft, and requefted a fpecimen of his art.   The three
firft examples were Barry, Woodward, and
Love, and happy would it have been for
Henderfon had he concluded there.   Mr.
Garrick appeared in extacy at the imitation ;
but, Sir, faid he, you'll kill poor Barry,
flay Woodward, and break Love's heart !
Your ear muft be wonderfully correct, and
your voice moft fingularly flexible—I am
told you *have me*.   Do, my dear Sir, let
me hear what I am, for if you are equally
exact with me as with Barry and Woodward,
I fhall know precifely what my peculiar tones

H 3

are—

are—*Henderson* excufed himfelf, by faying, that Mr. Garrick's powers were fuperior to imitation, that he would not prefume to attempt it, and begged leave to decline fo hazardous an undertaking, in which he was confcious any man *muft* fail; but the other two gentlemen preffing him to comply, he, " *in evil hour confented,*" and gave imitations from Benedict. The voice was fo exact as to delight the two auditors—But for Mr. Garrick; he fat in fullen filence for half a minute, then walked acrofs the room with an exclamation, " that egad, if, if, if that was his voice, he had never known it himfelf; for, upon his foul, it was entirely diffimilar to every thing he conceived *his* to be, and totally unlike any found that had ever ftruck upon his ear until that moment." So very unfair judges are we of whatever touches our own vanity, and fo fore at whatever wounds our own pride.

The

The great hero of the drama, the man upon whom, if we may believe Paul White-head, the taſte and virtue of a poliſhed nation depended,* could not bear to contemplate his own figure in the mirror which he often held up, and where he was delighted to view others.

Tremblingly alive, he ſhuddered at the ſhadow of ridicule, and felt as much from the apprehenſion of a paultry epigram by an obſcure news-paper ſcribbler, as Foote would have done from a volume of ſatire againſt himſelf, with the name of Churchill in the title page.

Who would wiſh to poſſeſs ſuch exceſs of irritability ? He ſeriouſly complained Mr.

H 4 Henderſon

---

* " A nation's taſte depends on you,

" Perhaps a nation's virtue too."

Henderson went about the town taking him off, and that he pofted him in every company.

A confcioufnefs of his own well-earned celebrity might have furnifhed him with fufficient armour againft fuch attacks, and upon many other occafions he feemed to poffefs this confcioufnefs in a very high degree.

Previous to this time, Mr. Pingo, by direction of Mr. Garrick, engraved a medal, on one fide of which was the manager's head. On the reverfe three figures, that refembled plague, peftilence, and famine, more than what they were intended to reprefent, namely *the three Graces,* with this modeft infcription,

"He has united all your powers."

This

This being by a gentleman to whom Mr. Garrick had prefented it; fhewn to Henderfon, when at my table with a number of his friends, he repeated the following little impromptu, which I think deferves the name of a good epigram.

Three fqualid hags, when Pingo form'd,
   And chriften'd them the *graces* ;
Garrick, with Shakefpeare's magic warm'd,
   Recogniz'd foon their faces.

He knew them for the fifters weird,
   Whofe art bedimm'd the noon-tide hour,
And from his lips this line was heard,
   " *I have united all your power.*"

So Garrick, critics all agree,
   The graces help'd thee to no riches,
And Pingo thus to flatter thee,
   Has made *his* graces wifhes.

. So long was this great man accuftomed to adulation, it became at laft neceffary to his dramatic exiftence, and fo eager was he to intercept the fhafts that were aimed againft him, that he held up to obferva- tion what would, without his interpofition, have fallen to the ground, and funk un- marked into oblivion. This might have been the fate of the imitations, but Mr. Garrick gave fome confequence to them, and the fpeaker, by his notice.*

Mr. Henderfon's friends had different opinions refpecting the propriety of mak-

ing

* I think it was Boerhaave, who being afked, why he did not write anfwers to fome pamphlets which were written againft his medical fyftem, replied, he thought of them as fparks upon the pages of his books, which he only had the power of blowing into a flame, but let alone they would go out of themfelves.

ing Mr. Garrick his model. I have inferted two letters, in which that circumftance is mentioned, written by a gentleman
who honoured him with his friendſhip
and protection, the firſt feaſon he played
at Bath.

To

To Mr. Henderson.

Bath, 27th June, 1773.

DEAR HENDERSON,

IF you had not wrote to me as you did, I fhould have concluded you had been laid down; pray, my boy, take care of yourfelf this hot weather, and don't run about London ftreets, fancying you are catching ftrokes of *nature*, at the hazard of your conftitution——It was my firft fchool, and deeply read in petticoats I am, therefore you may allow me to caution you.

Stick to Garrick as clofe as you can for your life: you fhould follow his heels like his fhadow in funfhine.

No

No one can be so near him as yourself when you please, and I'm sure when he sees it strongly as other people do, he must be fond of such an *ape*. You have nothing to do now but to stick to the few great ones of the earth, who seem to have offered you their assistance in bringing you to light, and to brush off all the low ones as fast as they light upon you. —You see I hazard the appearing a puppy in your eyes, by pretending to advise you, from the real regard, and sincere desire I have of seeing you a great and happy man. —Garrick is the greatest creature living in every respect, he is worth studying in every action.—Every view and every idea of him is worthy of being stored up for imitation, and I have ever found him a generous and sincere friend. Look upon him, Henderson, with your imitative eyes, for when he drops you'll have nothing but

poor

poor old nature's book to look in.—You'll be left to grope it out alone, ſcratching your pate in the dark, or by a farthing candle. — Now is your time, my lively fellow ——And do ye hear, don't eat ſo devi-liſh you'll get too fat when you reſt from playing, or get a ſudden jogg by illneſs to bring you down again. *   *
*   *   *   *   *   *   *

Adieu, my dear H,

believe me your's, &c.

T. G.

To Mr. HENDERSON.

Bath, July 18, 1773.

DEAR HENDERSON,

I F one may judge by your laft fpirited epiftle you are in good keeping, no one eats with a more grateful countenance, or fwallows with more good nature than yourfelf.

If this does not feem fenfe, do but recollect how many hard featured fellows there are in the world that frown in the midft of enjoyment, chew with unthankfulnefs, and feem to fwallow with pain inftead of pleafure ; now any one who fees you eat pig and plumb fauce, immediately *feels that pleafure* which a plump

morfel,

morſel, ſmoothly gliding through a narrow glib paſſage into the regions of blifs, and moiſtened with the dews of imagination, naturally creates.

Some iron-faced dogs you know ſeem to chew dry ingratitude, and ſwallow diſcontent. Let ſuch be kept to *under parts*, and never truſted to ſupport a character. —In all but eating ſtick to Garrick;— In *that* let him ſtick to you, for I'll be curſt if you are not his maſter.—Never mind the fools who talk of imitation and copying—All is imitation, and if you quit that natural likenefs to Garrick which your mother beſtowed upon you, you'll be flung ——Afk Garrick elfe.

Why, ſir, what makes the difference between man and man, is real performance, and

and not genius or conception.——There are a thoufand Garrick's, a thoufand Giardini's, and Fifher's, and Abels.   Why only one Garrick, with Garrick's eyes, voice, &c. &c. &c? One Giardini with Giardini's fingers, &c. &c.   But one Fifher with Fifher's dexterity, quicknefs, &c?   Or more than one Abel with Abel's feeling upon the inftrument?   All the reft of the world are mere *hearers* and *fee'ers*.

Now, as I faid in my laft, as nature feems to have intended the fame thing in you as in Garrick, no matter how fhort or how long, her kind intention muft not be croffed.————If it is, fhe will tip the wink to madam fortune, and you'll be kicked down ftairs.————

" Think on that Mafter Ford."

God blefs you,

I   T. G.

Mr. Garrick, however, as well as the other managers, frequently heard him rehearse both at his own houſe and upon the ſtage, treated him with polite attention, and acted with apparent kindneſs and good nature.

At one of theſe rehearſals was preſent Mr. George Garrick, who, being aſked if he would ſtay and hear Mr. Henderſon, ſaid he would do himſelf that pleaſure, *merely as a ſpectator*. But he found a very ſpeedy occaſion of objection, and ſaid that in one inſtance it appeared to him the ſpeaker miſtook the character. Egad, my dear Brother, ſaid Mr. Garrick, you moſt egregiouſly miſtake your own character; you told us juſt now you would remain a *Spectator*, you forget what you are, and turn *Tatler*; but never mind,

George,

George, Mr. Henderſon, whatever he is,
depend upon me being the *Guardian*.

Some of the other managers deigned
to think him *well enough* for Bath, but
totally unfit for the boards of a London
Theatre, and one of the players obſerved,
that, " Though he appeared a meteor in
the Bath *horizon*, he would be but a
farthing candle in the London *hemiſphere*."
The gentleman's meaning I am not bound
to explain, for it is not neceſſary for the
collector of a few ſcattered anecdotes to be
a philoſopher, but I dare ſay many of his
friends recollect the remark, for it was
made in the green-room.

Flattered by ſuch encomiums, and gratified by ſuch teſtimonies of approbation
from his brethren of the buſkin, on the

I 2.

24th

24th of September 1774, Mr. John Henderſon returned to Bath, to gather his ſecond crop of Somerſetſhire laurels.

During this ſeaſon he encreaſed his connections, ſtrengthened his reputation, and to the characters he had already performed, added thoſe of Zanga, Pierre, Don John, Sir John Brute, Bellville in the School for Wives, Henry the Second, Beverly in the Man of Buſineſs, Archer, Ranger, Comus, and Othello.

In the part of Othello I never ſaw him, but, by his own account, it was not ſuccefsful; and ſhall we wonder at his failure in that which eluded the graſp of Mr. Garrick. It was too mighty for him.

To Barry, the wonder working-Barry, and to him only, ſeemed to be given the

full

full powers for exhibiting the markings of this moſt difficult part.

" *But Barry's magic cannot copied be.*"

Amongſt the multitudes of candidates who have choſen to make their firſt appearance in this character, attracted, I believe, by its having, like Richard the Third, a ſonorous ſound, and giving them a power of maſking their terrors under a black face, how few have tolerably ſucceeded.

The Moor, is conceived with all the tremendous dignity of Shakeſpeare, and demands a portion of that fire which illumined the mighty maſter of the drama, to give him body and colouring to an audience.

I 3

Mr.

Mr. Henderſon informed me, that on his firſt appearance in Othello, the manager had habited him in ſo ridiculous a garb, that he wanted nothing but the bruſh and ſcraper, to give a compleat reſemblance of a chimney ſweeper on May-day, and that he was certain it exceeded all power of face, to avoid ſmiling at leaſt at ſo ludicrous a figure.

This diſconcerted him ſo much, as to check his effuſions, of which circumſtance, he never ſo totally loſt the recollection, as to appear in this character without ſome embarraſment.

That his want of ſucceſs was not owing to his want of application, will appear by the following letter to the Bath manager;

nager ; which fhould induce us to make every allowance for the errors of the performer in a new character, which he is frequently obliged to perfonate, without time for the proper and neceffary confideration,

I 4

To

To Mr. PALMER, at Bath.

London, August 3, 1773.

DEAR SIR,

I Have received Othello and your letters, to which I do not tell you that I will pay attention, but that *I am* attending to both. But it will be utterly impoffible that I fhould come down prepared for acting thofe parts you mention immediately. I never did, nor ever fhall repine, at the quantity, or the variety of bufinefs you employ me in, but furely it muft be for your intereft as well as my credit, to have me ftudied in the parts I am to appear in, and not to let me go on the ftage in the hafty, crude, and unpre-pared manner I have done. Mr. Garrick fays, " he has heard that I fwallowed my

parts

parts like an eager glutton, and ſpewed my undigeſted fragments in the face of the audience." The figure is nauſeous, but not more nauſeous than juſt.

You may be aſſured, my dear Sir, that I have no powers, or faculties of any ſort, which I would not exert in your ſervice. I may be deficient, but indolent I will never be. I muſt obſerve to you, that a thouſand incorrectneſſes, haſtineſſes, and errors, which the people excuſed in my firſt appearance, will not be ſo indulgently conſidered the ſecond ſeaſon, and for that reaſon I hope you will not expect I ſhould run through ſuch a haſty ſucceſſion of characters; and I hope too that you will conſider this obſervation not as an idle apology for lazineſs, but a ſerious appeal to your judgment and your friendſhip. It is ten to one but you laugh at this, but let me aſſure you, upon the

credit

credit of experience, that to keep ten or fifteen characters, of great magnitude, importance and variety, distinct and strong upon the mind and memory, is no trifling bufinefs. To learn words, indeed, is no great labour, and to pour them out no very difficult matter. It is done on our stage almost every night; but with what fuccefs, I leave you to judge. The generality of performers think it enough to learn the words, and thence all that vile uniformity and unvaried manner which difgraces the theatre.

I faw Mr. Garrick yefterday, and he has promifed to go over fome fcenes with me on Monday next.

As for *Othello*, I tremble at it: 'tis a mighty and an arduous tafk; but I begin to take great pleafure in it, and will bend it

to

to my powers, if I cannot raife them to it. But for God's fake, my dear friend, let me have time to weigh it well. Mr. Garrick affures me, he was upwards of two months rehearfing Benedict, before he could fatisfy himfelf that he had modelled his action and recital to his own idea of the part.

You will hurt me very much, if you think I have any vain or idle motives for what I fay. I do really feel that one ftrong and powerful idea in the mind for a while over-whelms and extrudes all others, and he who hopes to fucceed in Othello, or any part of fuch dignity and moment, muft give all his powers of thought and fancy to that, and that alone, till it is impreffed upon the me-mory ftrong enough to remain unfhaken by the ftreams of lighter images which pafs it. You will laugh, as we both did, at some-body elfe, if I intimate, it is for the honour

of

of your theatre that I wifh to tread it with the marks of thinking, and attention, and ftudy on me, and therefore I am content to folicit, as an indulgence to myfelf, that I may be allowed time to deliberate on my future characters. This I will venture to fay, you will not repent agreeing to my re-queft, for in the mind I am now in, I fee fo clearly the value of the reputation I hazard, that nothing can or fhall divert me from the moft fedulous application. As I write to the friend as well as the manager, I will add, that my induftry fhall have your advantage for part of its motive. I very fincerely hope Mrs. Palmer will recover her health, and you your happinefs. I have a moft perfect value and affection for you both, which, whether you either of you believe or not, I will ever preferve, and fo God blefs you.

Gainfborough

Gainſborough is a varlet, he promiſed me a miniature from the picture of mine, but wits and genius', if they get nothing elſe from the court, learn their d——d tricks of promiſing and forgetting. * * * * * *
* * * * * * * * * * * * * *

You are miſtaken in me. I fence almoſt every day, and ſtudy much, and eat little. I mean compared to your character of me. I think you had better write to Mr. Garrick about that lady. I have not ſeen Mrs. Greville, but have heard great things of her at Mr. G——s (the author), and from ſeveral others. I intend to go to Richmond this week.

J. H.

At

At the expiration of this second Bath season, with united testimonies of approbation from many who were deemed good judges of theatric merit, he returned to London, where he passed the few months of his recess. During this period, he frequently rehearsed, and read to Mr. Garrick, Mr. Foote*, Mr. Harris, and Mr. Leake, but

* At some of these rehearsals I was present, but Mr. Thomas Davies has given a description of one of them, in which he exhibits so true a picture of that most eccentric character, the late Sam Foote, that I hope I shall be pardoned for inserting it.

" Before Henderson left London, he was advised to try if Mr. Foote would not give him an opportunity of shewing himself at his theatre in the Haymarket. Two friends accompanied him to North End. Our modern Aristophanes welcomed the visitants with great civility ; but such is the volatility of his genius, that it was not possible to announce the errand immediately : he must be

permitted

but his fate was to find all of them,
" Damn with faint praise."

It

permitted to indulge his peculiar humour, and to let off
a few voluntaries, before he could be induced to hear of
any bufinefs whatfoever.   Foote's imagination is fo
lively, and his conceptions fo rapid, as well as exuberant,
that his converfation is a cataract, or torrent of wit, humour, pleafantry, and fatire.   The company had fcarce
unfolded their bufinefs, when he gave them the hiftory
of Sir Gregory Grinwell and Lady Barbary Bramble.
The whimfical fituations into which he put his characters
with his lively and farcaftic remarks, threw the company into convulfions of laughter.

" However, Henderfon's friends thought it was now
time to ftop the current of Mr. Foote's vivacities, by
informing him of the reafon of their vifit.   One of
them took the lead :—

" Sir, our young friend, the Bath Rofcius, would
think himfelf extremely happy to have the opinion of fo
acknowledged a judge of theatrical merit as you are ;

he

It was, however, the earneſt wiſh of his friends, that he ſhould appear upon the London

he wiſhes you would permit him to rehearſe a ſcene of a play."

" Well, Sir, what are you for, the ſock or the buſkin? I'll be hanged if you are not quite enamoured of that bouncing brimſtone Tragedy."—Mr. Henderſon is not confined, Sir, to either.—" Stick to the ſock, young gentleman; the one is all nature, and the other all art and trick. Tragedy is mere theatrical bombaſt, the very fungus of the theatre. Come, Sir, give us a taſte of your quality."—Here Henderſon began a ſpeech in Hamlet; when Foote, turning round to one of the company, ſaid, " Have you not heard in what manner this impudent little ſcoundrel has treated me?"—" I proteſt, Sir, I don't know whom you mean."—" No, where have you left your apprehenſion? Let me but tell you what a damned trick he ſerved me lately, by lending me a large ſum of money."—" Conſider, my dear Sir, the time grows late, and we are to dine in town."— " No, no," ſaid Foote, " you ſhall dine with me upon a ſtewed

London ſtage, and try if the public would
be more indulgent than the directors of their
amuſements;

a ſtewed rump of beef, and a diſh of fiſh." Now Mr.
Henderſon begins. Well, once more he endeavoured
to open, when behold, an unlucky joke, *a petite hiſtoire*,
ſome droll thought, or ſome unaccountable idea, prevented the diſconcerted actor from diſplaying his powers
of elocution: his caſe was now become extremely
pitiable.

However, after hearing this ſingular genius read an
act of his new comedy, take off Lady Betty Biggamy,
recite the whole trial of himſelf and George Faulkener,
ridicule the Iriſh Lord Chief Juſtice Robinſon, for con-
demning his Peter Paragraph for a libel, ſpeak a Prologue in the character of Peter, laugh at our moſt celebrated orators of the bar, mimic the members of both
Houſes of Parliament, tell ſome ludicrous ſtories of Cap-
tain Bodens and the Iriſh chairman, Henderſon was
permitted to repeat, without interruption, Mr. Garrick's
Prologue, which he ſpoke on his firſt appearance, after
his arrival from the Continent. This being no cari-

K

cature,

amufements; but this ftep he himfelf was not very earneft to take, unlefs he could be received upon terms, which it was not very eafy to procure. By *terms,* I do not mean falary; that was not the principal object, but

cature, but a genuine and fair reprefentation of the great Rofcius's manner, without the leaft exaggeration, we cannot be furprifed that it did not make any impreffion upon Mr. Foote; however, he paid the fpeaker a compliment upon the goodnefs of his ear. Dinner was now announced; every thing was princely, and in fplendid order. Wit flew about the table : I mean Mr. Foote's; for I would advife every man that has any wit of his own, who fhall have the honour to dine with this gentleman, to bottle it up for another occafion; for he is himfelf mafter of enough, and to fpare, for ten companies. I need not obferve that many portraits were drawn, and fome of them in a mafterly ftile.

When Henderfon took his leave of him, he whifpered one of the company in the ear, " *that he would not do.*" Mr. Foote confirmed the death-warrant that had been already figned by *Garrick, Colman, Harris,* and *Leake.*

but exemption from being forced upon characters for which he was unqualified, in
which his confequent failure would have
blighted his budding honours, and funk
him into the obfcurity he fo much dreaded.
Somewhat chagrined at the reception which
had been given him by the monarchs of the
theatre, in September, 1774, he returned
to Bath.

That his mortification had not wholly
fubdued his pleafantry, appears from the
following letter, which he wrote a few days
previous to his leaving London, to a friend
who was then at Margate.

To

To Mr. I———.

London, Sept. 21, 1774.

A S there is an exprefs coming to thee, I fhall write, otherwife it would not have been worth thy while to have paid a groat for what thou haft fo often paid for before, and that is my love. I hope thou art become an inhabitant of the deep waters by this time, and wilt give me an account of the vegetation of coral, and the venereal amufements of fharks and lampreys;—fay nothing to the women, but tell me privately, whether the porpoife hath that amorous alacrity which the fat ones of the earth fo much wonder at, and whether there be any fuch thing as conjugal fidelity among the herrings and the lobfters of the ocean. As for the reft, thanks for the draft, which I fhall not ufe,

becaufe

becauſe foreſeeing that the waves would cling longer about your waiſt than you at firſt imagined, I applied to your friend H.

Adieu,

J. HENDERSON.

P. S.   I ſet out from your houſe for Bath on Sunday morning. My week's buſineſs is as follows : Monday, Hamlet ; Tueſ-day, Benedict ; Wedneſday, Belville.

K 3

His

His reception at Bath was in the higheſt degree gratifying. Men, to whoſe deciſions the world paid implicit obedience, diſtinguiſhed his talents, invited him to their tables, and admitted him as the companion of their feſtive hours, where his eaſy humour and lively pleaſantry enſured him a moſt welcome reception. But this pleaſantry was not ſufficiently guarded. In the hours of merriment and laughter, he was often aſked for imitations, and Mr. Garrick being the *Magnus Apollo* of the drama, whoſe actions were obvious to all, and of whoſe manners no one was ignorant, Mr. Henderſon was frequently requeſted to exhibit him. The inconveniences he had formerly felt had not taught him caution; he continued the ſame practice, and with more accuracy than prudence, gave the little ſtories of the day, and entered ſo forcibly into the manner of that great man, that

every

every hearer was ſtruck with the reſemblance. This was a freedom Mr. Garrick could not forgive. For a young theatrical adventurer, upon a country ſtage, and conſequently dependant upon him for an introduction to Drury-lane, to make *his* peculiarities the object of imitation, was a ſin never to be forgiven, and perhaps one ſource of the difficulties he found, in his attempts at an introduction to a London theatre.

At Bath he, however, encreaſed his dramatic reputation, and performed in either play or farce, four or five times a week. He added to his liſt of characters, amongſt many others, thoſe of Ford, Poſthumus, Shylock, Lorenzo in the Spaniſh Friar, Sciolto, and Morcar in Matilda.

Many of his friends thought he was waſting that time at Bath which might be

K 4

employed

employed, with more advantage to his purse, and without hazard to his reputation, in London; but he himself reasoned somewhat differently, and, in this instance, evinced, that a cautious prudence, a quick eye to what constituted his own interest, and a persevering judgment to pursue it, were strong *traits* in his character.

The newspapers of the day gave a very serious recital of this business, with all the dignity of history, and all the air of authority; but as these grave writers were not perfectly masters of *data* on which to ground their arguments, they have censured him for errors of which he was not guilty, and defended motives by which he was not actuated.

His

His own reasonings may, I should apprehend, best appear from his own letters, written to different friends, with whom he then lived in habits of the most unreserved confidence.

To

To Mr. I———,

Bath, October 24th, 1772.

MY MOST DEAR FRIEND,

D O N ' T think me careleſs of your advice, or of my own affairs, becauſe I did not write to you by return of the poſt. The importance of the matter, made ſtill more important by your inter-ference, reſolved me to think moſt deliber-ately and attentively on it, before I formed my concluſions.—I have now, I think, conſidered it amply, and compared the advantages with the hazards—you will be convinced, that no *money intereſts* have influence on my deciſions, when I tell you, that I have reſolved to ſtay here ſome time longer.—" What has then ?" you will aſk.

—Reputation.

—Reputation.—" Reputation, fay you, my good friend, why that will be loft in Bath, and London will eftablifh it." I think not fo, and I will tell you why. Nothwithftanding I have played forty parts here, there are not more than five or fix which I dare offer to a London audience, on account of the fame I *have* acquired.—So fmall a number will not carry me through a feafon, and if they would, I could not have them to myfelf, becaufe I fhould not be allowed to keep even thofe parts, as it is a rule in London, not to difpoffefs any performer of thofe characters which he is thought in any degree to deferve to fupport.—I muft then be forced upon others in which I have no merit, or none that will fupport the name I have got, and you would have the mortification to fee your friend finking into infignificance, and living a kind of rent-charge upon the Theatre.

atre. No advantage of *benefit* whatever would compenſate *that.* The reaſons I give for ſtaying here, are, I think, powerful ones. I am not ripe enough for London, and what a fool of a gardener would he be who ſhould ſend a baſket of *green* peaches to market, when, if he had ſtayed a little while longer, he might have ſent them ripened and rich flavoured. *" A fooliſh figure, but farewell it, for I will uſe no art."*——You Jack, and myſelf, and all my friends, have miſtaken my talents—we uſed to think that their livelineſs and vigour would force them into reputation, but I find now that they require the moſt ſedulous correction—In ſhort, I muſt ſtudy, and I will make this place my college, 'till I have brought my talents to be much more like perfection than they are at preſent, that you and the reſt

of

of my friends need not blush at the encomiums you have either silently, or openly,
bestowed upon me. If you was to see
me play Hamlet now, you would scarce
know it to be the same person you saw
before, and those who *do* see it *now*, will,
I hope, soon be convinced that they shall
see it still better. It is a real truth, that
I feel my mind enlarges, and my powers
invigorate very sensibly—you'll say, would
they not do the same in London?——I
answer, *no*. The continual practice I am
in here is of great advantage to me—I once
thought it an hardship to be forced upon
so many characters, I think so now no
longer, being convinced that almost every
part I play, however unsuited to my nature, and however ill I may appear in it,
does me good; in London it would do
me harm; for this reason : there are com-

puted

puted to be *thirty* different audiences in London, here there are but *two* at the utmost, and those of them who see me to a disadvantage one night, see me to advantage the *next*.—I appeal to the world whether I am losing myself here.

As to salary, that will be raised, and Palmer has told me, that a bank-note of fifty pounds is ready for me, when I please, for my services last year. I will soon convince you, my kindest friend, that I want no money—It is true that I have not any, but consider, I am a student—when I have gone through my classes, and can give a good translation of Shake-speare to the world I will publish it, and I will present you with a copy, bound and gilt, if not lettered, in as good a calves-skin as I can procure.

Adieu,

Adieu——I will reply to the other parts of your letter when I have more leifure.

J. HENDERSON.

To

Bath, 22*d December*, 1774.

I AM fure by your letter that it was written in the very fpirit of friendfhip, and I have not been more gratified a great while than in reading it. I thank you moft earneftly for your concern and attention to my interefts : to fhew you what confidence I have in your fincerity and *fecrefy*, (though the foolifh world will not allow that virtue to your fex) I will explain to you more private and perfonal reafons for my not being eager to come to London, than I have written to E———, or to my deareft J———? They are not for the world to know, and E——— and Jack may fhew

my

my letters to them, to all the world, *by my choice.*

You are to know then that I think Mr. Garrick has acted very *illiberally* and *ungentlemanly* in my regard.———I will tell you *how.* Mr. C———d sent to me the other morning, after my playing Benedict, to compliment and applaud me. He told me that he was astonished at my performance, that Mr. Garrick had prepared him for a very different opinion.—— Mr. C———d then shewed me a letter from him, wherein he says, " See Henderson more than once, and give me your real opinion of him."——Mr. C———d did so, and that opinion was the most kind and favourable that could be imagined. Yet Mr. G——— took no manner of notice of it, though he constantly wrote to Mr. C———d. Mr. Garrick then

L

tampers

tampers with E——————, whom you know
the honour of being thought of Mr. Garrick's counfel would incline to any thing,
He immediately tells Jack and my friends
what a favourable opportunity there is for
me, and they, eager to ferve me, think
I fhould jump at it. Mr. Garrick, then,
to ufe a fcripture phrafe, " *Ploughs with
my heifer.*"——————Now the fcheme appears to
me thus in Mr. G——————'s plan.—————— Let
Henderfon be tempted by his friends, and
by his own ambition, to come to London,
he will then *apply to me*, and I can make
my own conditions, he will then be confidered as one whom I patronize, and protect; whereas if I apply to *him*, he will
make conditions with *me*, and from my
acknowledging the *want* of him, I cannot have him at *my beck*.

I did

I did not however fwallow the bait fo greedily as was imagined; and the confequence is that Mr. George Garrick has applied to me, but for the reafons I have written my dear I———, I declined his offer. When I talk of conditions, I defire to be underftood, my friend, that I do not mean *pecuniary* ones, if they had been my object I fhould not ftay *here*. To give you ftill farther proof that they are not, Mr. C.———d told me the other night, that he was afhamed of the part Mr. Garrick had acted in this affair, and that he would undertake to get me whatever terms I pleafed at Covent-Garden, which, he added, was the houfe I muft think of whenever I came to London. * * *
* * * * * * * * * * * * *
* * * * * * * * * * * *. He wifhes too, he fays, that I would not make my engagement for fo long as *three*

                    years,

years, but I ought not to regard that, becaufe *if I make myfelf of real importance,* the forfeiture of my articles will be no impediment to my leaving Bath, and if I do not make myfelf of real importance, neither you nor any real friend will wifh to fee me there.

As to pofting Mr. Garrick, I have explained the whole affair to George Garrick, who was fatisfied, and Palmer wrote to Mr. G. to take the whole fault upon himfelf, if there was any fault. So that Mr. Garrick cannot be difpleafed with me. * * * * * * * * * *. ————I hope a little time will convince you that I am right.

Mr. C————d behaves to me with remarkable complaifance and refpect, and laft night, after my playing Shylock, he

came

came to me, and faid that he was forry he could not ftay here long enough to intereft himfelf at my benefit, that he fhould regret leaving Bath without giving fome inftance of the refpect he had for my genius, and return for the pleafure it had given him, he therefore offered me a new Tragedy for my benefit, if I thought it would advantage me.

Since this is a letter of private fentiments, you muft allow me to indulge a little vanity, and pleafe myfelf with telling you, that Lord N———m, a nobleman who commands the tafte of a numerous party of literati, and of wits, &c, came behind the fcenes to me laft night, with two other gentlemen, to thank me for my Shylock, and his lordfhip was pleafed to fay, it was the moft finifhed piece of acting he ever faw, and that it far exceeded Macklin's.

In

In one word——if I thought I should never be a better actor than I am, I would not hesitate to be in London, but I will endeavour to make myself respectable and important before I come.

I hope, my very dear friend, that you see my conduct and my reasoning in a right point of view, and I flatter myself there is some resolution and firmness in my mind, since I can resist so alluring a temptation, and

" *Stick to poverty with peace of mind.*"

Declamations, are often and reasonably suspected of having no other motive than the glitter of period, or the loftiness of language, but I *act*, as well as argue.

God

God bleſs you, my good girl, I have written to an immeaſureable length, but I would have you poſſeſſed of my reaſons for the ſeeming negligence of my conduct in this affair.

J. HENDERSON.

To

Bath, Dec. 26, 1774.

SOMEHOW or other, my dear Jack, neither you nor Mrs. I—— fee this affair right. In the firft place, Garrick did not defire E——s to bid me make my own pro-pofal, or if he did, E——s did not explain that to me. Thefe are his words—" I faw Mr. Garrick this afternoon; we talked of you. He afked me, if you wifhed to play the enfuing winter at Drury-lane, and if fo, why you did not write to him; that if you two could agree, *" he was ready to engage you."*

In the next place, ye are wrong in fup-pofing that Mr. George Garrick *called on me ; he did not.* I met him in the ftreet, and

and that morning a paragraph had appeared in the Bath papers concerning my having refolved to renew my engagements here. Mr. George Garrick's words to me, after the firft falutations, were, as nearly as I can recollect: " I had a letter from my brother, defiring me to call upon you, and hear if you had any thing to propofe for the next winter, but as I fee by the papers you have engaged again here, *it is very well.*" I replied, that I had not figned articles, but that I had almoft promifed Mr. Palmer to ftay with him, becaufe I thought this a very proper *fchool* for me—I then explained to him the nature of the miftake about *pofting* his brother, and we parted.

I wonder you can think *I bear myfelf too high,* when I confent to ftay here a poor provincial, when I might be at a

theatre

theatre in London. I can quote as well as you :

———" *Thou keep'ſt me from the light.*"

Again,

" *I'm ſharing ſpoil before the field is won* ;
" *Clarence ſtill breathes, Edward ſtill lives and reigns,*
" When they are *gone*, then muſt *I* count my gains."

I have this morning had converſation with Mr. Cumberland; he adviſes me to engage here, but only to engage from year to year— he promiſes to procure me an engagement at either theatre, equal to that of *Smith*, or *Reddiſh*, or *Lee*. The only dread I have, is, that of being put upon inferior charac-ters—'till Garrick leaves the ſtage, I *muſt* at his theatre. There is more in the poſ-ſeſſion of characters than you ſeem to think. Mr. G. Garrick himſelf told Mr. C——d, that I ſhould have *two trial parts*, but they

afterwards

afterwards muſt devolve to their preſent poſ-
ſeſſors. Do only, my beloved friend, think
what I muſt do *then*.

You know, whilſt you urge the *town* as
a reaſon to me, that the town do not inter-
fere. How was *Lee*, whom you will allow
to have merit, and who *had* more than he
has, I believe; how, I ſay, was he forced
upon inſignificant parts? I have ſeen his
name in the bills for *Don John*, in *Much
Ado about Nothing*.

What is urged as to my being under
Mr. Garrick's directions, with regard to improvement, is a very powerful argument
with me not to be with him. I have been
this two years labouring to loſe the reſemblance of him, which had like to have
ruined me for ever, and ſtamped me with
the diſgrace of mimickry, and now if I was

with

with him, I should *re*-gain all that would confirm that character to the world, and in my best of praise should be called a very good *copy*. I shall see Mr. C——d after the play this evening, and then I will write more. I shall stipulate with Palmer, that I will play only on such nights as the company, I mean the gentry, are expected, and to relinquish some certain characters, and only to engage from year to year. It is the opinion of my Lord Newnham, and many of my friends of that rank in life, that I ought not to go to London while Garrick is there.

I am but just beginning to be talked of——Parties will, in time, be made in my favour by people of *rank* and *power*, but it must be done by time—the protection and the influence of five or six noblemen, will avail me more than any thing ; however, I

have

have commiffioned Mr. C——d to nego-
ciate for me, fo far as to know Mr. Garrick's real intentions towards me, but on
no terms whatever will I confent to be liable
to infignificant characters. You cannot,
my dear Jack, you cannot imagine, how
foon I might be ruined in London, if I am
in the power of thofe who meditate my
ruin—for God's fake, only confider what an
irrecoverable fhock it would be to be obliged
to return to Bath, or to lay at the back of
the theatre on a falary of *bounty* more than
merit. As to Mr. Garrick's patronage and
friendfhip, I have no right to expect it. If
Mr. G—— had meant to patronize me, he
would have done it at *firft*, and not have
fent me to this place, which, though it was
as prudent a meafure as could be planned
for me, I really believe Mr. Garrick *did not
confider*. My reafons for this belief, are,
that he conftantly fpeaks in my difcredit, to
thofe.

thofe whom he ever fpeaks to at all about me. A circumftance which you fhould con-fider maturely *as I have done.* The cafe is fimply this: I *have* great merit, or I *have* *not.* If I have, it fhould entitle me to a refpectable confideration. If I have *not*, I ought not to be feen in London, and lofe the fame I have there. Oh! but fay you and Mrs. I——, " Shandy, why will you be fo proud, there is a fecond rate fame and profit in the theatre, with which you fhould be content as yet"—I do not think fo. ——" Th' afpiring blood of Lancafter has not funk in the ground."† My talents

are

† The letter, to which this is an anfwer, began with the following quotation:—

——" What!
" Will th' afpiring blood of Lancafter fink in the
     ground?
" I thought it would have mounted."

are not of that caft; though I have acquired
great reputation in *Richard*, I fhould make
a very infignificant figure in his good coufin
of Buckingham. Hamlet too would fupport *me*, but I could never fupport *Horatio*,
and fo on.

J. H.

To Mr. I————.

Bath, Jan. 2, 1775.

DEAR FRIEND,

IN confequence of the letter I told you I wrote to Mr. Garrick, upon which fubject alfo Mr. Taylor wrote, Mr. Garrick writes thus to Mr. Taylor.

" Dear Sir,

" I received laft night a letter from you,
" and another from Mr. Henderfon, upon
" the fame fubject—I fhall therefore beg,
" that this anfwer to you may ferve for both.
" In my opinion, your propofal would be
" a very injurious one to Mr. Henderfon—
" can he or you believe, that his playing

" only

" only twice, a different character too each
" time, would give the public a proper idea
" of his merit?——The diffidence and ap-
" prehenfion, natural to a performer of feel-
" ing, might make him incapable of fhew-
" ing his talents and powers the firft time
" upon a new ftage, and upon which the
" great and eftablifhed eftimate muft be
" put upon his merit; fhould his fears
" prevail too much, which are ever ftrongeft
" with actors of keeneft fenfibility, he
" might be effentially hurt—could Mr.
" H. have an opportunity of performing
" ten or twelve different characters, his ge-
" nius would have fair play, otherwife, as
" his well-wifher, I proteft againft the
" other fcheme.   *   *   *   *
*   *   *   *   *   *   *
*   *   *   *   *   *.

M   " If

" If Mr. H. chufes to be with me,
" why fhould he not chufe three parts,
" Hamlet, Shylock, Benedick, or what he
" pleafes to appear in next feafon, and to
" have elbow room to difplay all his tra-
" gick and comick powers. I will either
" come into *certain* terms with him, or
" *conditional*, as he and his friends pleafe.
" I can fay no more, or offer any thing
" fairer, or more for his intereft.—I pro-
" teft againft the other partial manner of
" trial, which can be of no fervice to the
" manager, and may be of great prejudice
" Mr. Henderfon.

I am,

Dear Sir,

Yours, &c.

D. GARRICK.

Now, Jack, you know as much of the matter as I do.—What fhall I do?—What propofals fhall I make, and what anfwer fhall I give?—You know very well, and fo do all my friends, that the fpirit of my defign to ftay in Bath was to make myfelf mafter of fuch a *number of principal cha- racters*, as would fecure me from the dan- ger of being employed in infignificant or improper ones; by *improper*, I mean fuch, as however important or reputable, do not come within the compafs of my abilities; fuch for inftance is Romeo, &c.—By being put into either, I conceive the little fame I have got would be ruined, and I fhould be in a much worfe fituation than if I had never ventured upon the ftage. Mr. Garrick's letter indeed now feems to open me a fecurity from that danger, and in my own mind I would leave to him *all other terms*, than thofe of *choofing my characters.*

M 2

I care

I care not how often I play, but Mr. Garrick may be led in his candour to imagine, I have fucceeded in more characters than I really have.—Do, my dear Jack, lay this before my friends, and *confult and determine for me*. I fay this not becaufe I think your own decifion infufficient, but becaufe I hate to write the fame letters to different people—there you fee I have the honour to refemble Mr. Garrick.

J. H.

To

To Mr. I————.

Bath, January 23, 1775.

AS I find that lady has told you fome circumftances about my negotiation with Mr.
Garrick, I now fend you more. I wrote,
indeed, by the very next poft, to defire her
not to acquaint you with any part of it 'till
fhe heard farther from me, becaufe I had a
letter from Mr. C————d, which feemed to
open a new negotiation. I have not time to
copy it here, but its purport was, that *he*
wifhed the *paft differences* might be forgot,
and the curtain dropped; I wrote in anfwer,
that " I was very willing to forget all that
had paft; but that fuppofing the curtain *was*
dropped, the power of raifing it, and open-
ing a new fcene of negotiation, was not in
me; that, if through Mr. Cumberland's

M 3

means,

means, or by Mr. Garrick's own directions, any propofals were made to me, I would give a fpeedy and direct anfwer."

In confequence of this, I this morning received a letter, written by Mr. Garrick to Mr. C——d, wherein he fays :——

" I cannot alter my opinion of Mr. H——n's propofals, but I fay no more of them ; – you feem to wifh he fhould make his appearance upon our ftage—As I have not feen him act, and cannot guefs at his merit, which is fo varioufly fpoken of, I will agree that Mr. Henderfon fhall perform any two parts at the beginning of next feafon, which he fhall pleafe to fix upon, and afterwards upon others that we fhall both agree upon. After he has performed ten or twelve times, and the public voice will be known, two gentlemen, one chofen

by

by him, and one by me, fhall fix upon his falary for the feafon ; but, upon their dif-agreement, a third may be called in, and he muft determine the difference.

" To make fomething certain for Mr. Henderfon and the referrees to go upon, fuppofe we agree that his falary fhall not be lefs than *five* pounds a week, nor more than *ten*, for the feafon, with a benefit. After his falary is fixed, he muft become like the other performers, fubject to my manage-ment *wholly*."

It will not be neceffary to copy Mr. C——d's letter to me—he advifes the fcheme, and thinks I fhall be *fafe in the experiment*.

Now, my dear Jack, you muft know, that *five* pounds a week in London, is not

 much

much more than *four* pounds here, becaufe *we* are paid every week, from the beginning of our feafon 'till the end of it, alike; whereas in London, *all Lent*, and during thofe weeks in which the houfe is open only *three nights* in the week, the pay is but *half*.—Obferve, that Garrick only propofes to engage me one year, and at the end of that he might difgrace or lower me at his pleafure. If I ftay with Palmer, I engage for *three years*, and have three guineas a week—befides the advantage of the Improvement that conftant acting of capital parts muft unavoidably give me.

Mr. Taylor is now in London, and I have juft had a letter from him, wherein he fays, after having feen Mr. Garrick play, " Depend upon it you will be received whenever Garrick retires from the ftage, with great *eclat*; I am more convinced of that *now*

than

than ever. It will not do for you to attempt rifing on the ftage as they do in the
army and navy, by feniority; you muft come
out at once a comet, and not be content
with appearing as a twinkling ftar, liable to
be obfcured by every little cloud that flies
before you. To drop the metaphor, your
talents muft be fo well improved and ripened,
that any flight imperfections will be inftantly
overlooked, and your friends, the judges and
true critics, be able to bear down the ill-
natured remarks which will always attend
true merit."

I am fure, my moft dear, my moft worthy
friend, I fhall impofe a grateful tafk upon
you, when I beg you to vifit Mr. Taylor at
his brother's houfe, and talk the matter over
with him. I fhall write by this poft to
prepare him for your vifit, and afterwards

fend

ſend me with all the ſpeed you can; your opinion and advice.

You can have no conception of the anxiety of my mind in this affair. I dread London, I dread Garrick, I dread myſelf.

I truſt you with all the vanities of my heart, and will therefore ſend you the be-ginnings of thoſe letters I made to you. You will ſee by their dates how I ad-dreſſed you. There is no time, no hour hardly, in which I do not think of you with the ſincereſt and moſt ſolicitous regard.

God bleſs you—I have not time to cor-rect what I have written.

J. HENDERSON.

With

With Henderſon's conduct, in the courſe of the foregoing tranſactions, Mr. Garrick was highly offended; accuſed him of an inſolent attempt to uſurp his province, take the management out of his hands, and dictate ſuch terms as no actor of the moſt eſtabliſhed reputation had ever preſumed to offer. This accuſation Mr. Henderſon warmly diſclaimed; declaring, that the only motives which influenced him, were, that attention to his own fame which every man ought to preſerve, and that attention to his own ſafety which the frequent conduct of managers to performers, gave ſome reaſon for; and which his duty to a public, who had honoured him by their approbation, to his friends, who had diſtinguiſhed him by their partiality, and to himſelf, fully juſtified. This reaſoning had no effect upon Mr. Garrick, and the hopes of an engagement at Drury-lane, were for the preſent

wholly

wholly given up. But one of his friends, wishing him in a situation where his talents would have the encouragement they deserved, made application to Mr. Harris, who appeared pleased at the overture, and eager to engage him, which Henderson being informed, offered his services upon the same terms which had been prescribed by Mr. Garrick, and received for answer, that if he had any thoughts of continuing with Mr. Palmer, the London manager would by no means, come between them, whatever might be the eventual advantage to Covent-garden Theatre, and without waiting for an answer from Henderson, though he might possibly have heard from his friend Mr. Palmer, absolutely declined entering into any treaty with him, let the result of the Bath business, then pending, be what it would.

This

This feemed to bar the door of Covent-garden Theatre, and his firft determination was to quit Bath, and pafs a few months in France; but a prudent attention to his own intereft, and the confequent timidity of mind, which dreaded being without an engagement, operated fo far, that he entered into a new agreement with the Bath manager.

To

Bath, 24th Feb. 1775.

D I D not my narrative inform you that I had pofitively refufed ftaying with P————If you have not obferved it then, I do affure you now that *I have*. I fent it him in writing, and I will hold my promife to you and my friends,

I have not the leaft doubt but P———r hath obftructed my engagement at Covent-Garden,

" And will no doubt with reafons anfwer it,
" For Brutus is an *honourable man,*
" So are they *all, all honourable men.*"

I certainly

I certainly will do as you advise, and I think myself very happy that I have such counsellors as I cannot oppose without forfeiting all difcretion, or good fenfe. —This is a ftrange turned phrafe, but I take as much pains to avoid writing in a ftrain of compliment to you, as fome would to affect it, not becaufe *I* think that civility and truth can be feldom united, for there again *you* act fo that there is no feparating them, but that I would not have you hum over thofe parts of my letter as carelefs as you do thofe of any other perfon, who celebrates your wit or your good fenfe, or your good nature, which I know you always think it better to *poffefs* than to hear of.

Here you may take a pinch of fnuff.

I am

I am advifed, on all hands, to pafs this enfuing fummer in France, in order to fteal their receipt for making *incenfe*, and other materials, which, on my return, I may ufe on my theatrical altar, and make a folemn facrifice to the *Graces*. This I fhall certainly do; for though I know very well that all the ingredients may be bought in London, and cheaper too, than in France, yet I confider myfelf as a merchant who muft obey the commiffions of his correfpondents, and fend them whatever they demand from whatever fhore they direct.

I affure you, my dear friend, that ever fince I gave P——r a pofitive anfwer, my mind has been in conftant ferenity and compofure.——I mean in all regards of future engagements, and I conftantly reply, when any friends afk me how I can be fo weak

as

as to throw myfelf out of all employment, that I muſt take my chance, and I ſay it with moſt unaffected indifference.

Pray have you ſeen my picture at Gainf-borough's yet.—If not, why don't you go?—I intend it for my deareſt Jack, becauſe I think it very like, and he who hath known my heart for ſo many years, hath the beſt title to my reſemblance.

I wiſh you had ſeen me play Hamlet the other night.—*Vanity!*—Oh, you ſim-pleton!——It was becauſe I ſhould have ſeen *you here*.

If you make any more excuſes about your writing, I will cut them out of your letters, for they have no buſineſs there, and ſend them back—beſides every excuſe is an intruder, and takes up that room,

N   which

which I can prove by the other parts of
your letters, would have contained much
good humour and kindneſs and good writing,
by which it is manifeſt you have cheated
me ; and it is an aggravation of your crime,
that you have ſingled me out to impoſe
upon from a large circle of people, who
are all ready to ſwear that you never acted
otherwiſe to them than with the moſt up-
right integrity. I repeat, that it is particularly cruel and unjuſt in you to treat me
ſo, who am, as much as any of them can
be for their ſouls,

Your very ſincere and faithful,

J. HENDERSON.

During the summer of 1775 he performed with Mr. Reddish at Bristol, where
from the accidental indisposition of a performer, he on the seventeenth of August
played Falstaff, a character which nature
seemed to have forbade by every external
disqualification. But the difficulty increased
the honour, and success justified the undertaking.

It would degrade his memory, to compare him with any one who ever personated this *mountain of delight*, except Mr.
Quin, who appeared mentally and corpo-
really formed for the character.

The first play I ever saw was Henry the
Fourth, when Quin performed Falstaff, it
being, I think, the last time he ap-

peared

peared on the ſtage, for the benefit of Mr. Ryan.

Of his playing I have not any recollection, but in the ſcene of the battle, inſtead of the ſtump of a tree on which Falſtaff ſits to reſt himſelf, I remember the then directors of the Theatre introduced a crimſon velvet arm chair, with gilt claw feet and blue fringe.

I have been told by thoſe who have a perfect remembrance of the veteran's performance, that it was more important, but leſs pleaſant than Henderſon's, who had alſo the ſuperiority in the ſoliloquies, but that where the old knight aſſumes dignity, Quin's ſurly humour was beyond competition.

In

In the summer of 1776, he played under the management of Mr. Yates at Birmingham, and here first saw that meteor of the drama, Mrs. *Siddons,* who, the preceding season, had performed *Portia, Lady Anne,* and a few other characters at Drury-Lane, but with so little *eclat,* that upon Mr. Garrick's retiring, the succeeding managers not thinking her merits equal to a very trifling salary, she was discharged for inability ! ! !

Of her talents Mr. Henderson entertained the most exalted opinion, and wrote to Mr. Palmer, recommending him in the strongest terms to engage her, but he having already a person under articles, who had a similar cast of characters, the recommendation was at that time without effect. Yet, who that has seen Mrs. Siddons, will withhold their sanction to Mr. Henderson's judgment.

It

It may be almoſt ſaid of her, that, *as an actreſs*, ſhe has all the various merit which was poſſeſſed by any daughter of the tragic muſe who ever trod the Engliſh ſtage, and all the various merit which they wanted.

At the commencement of the ſeaſon he returned to Bath; a critique upon his per-formance, under the ſignature of the Lon-don Rider, appearing in the Morning Chro-nicle, he notices it in the following letter.

To

To the Rev. Mr. D———.

DEAR FRIEND,

I THANK you very heartily for your letter; it confirms me in all that I have thought of your candour and your friend-ship, which I have loved and honoured ever since I was capable of loving and ho-nouring any thing as I ought.———I won-der you should think I was abused by the *London Rider*, who, whatever his intentions may be, has paid me the highest compli-ment.—His objections to me were, that I imitated Garrick in *Sciolto,* and imitated him in the worst parts, his guttural sounds, &c. Now it is certain I never saw Garrick

in

in Sciolto, and if I had, that thickneſs
and feebleneſs he complains of were not
improper for the *age* of Sciolto.———The
Rider doth not complain of thoſe defects
in Comus, in Lorenzo, in Falſtaff, which
certainly are not like Garrick's manner.
He only finds that they are, where I think
they ought to be, in an old and diſtreſſed
man.—He finds indeed that I have not dignity—he finds alſo that I have not gentility
enough for the gay Lorenzo, whom Elvira
is to fall in love with at the firſt ſight,
though I think he allows me ſome portion of eaſe and ſprightlineſs.—He finds
alſo that I have not an eye for the jocund
and voluptuous Falſtaff—I cannot help it,
but I have, without vanity, juſt ſuch an
eye as the *Poet* has aſſigned that character
———" Do you ſet down your name in the
" ſcrowl of youth," ſays the Chief Juſtice
to Falſtaff, " that are written down *old*,
with

with all the characters of age?—Have you not a *moist* eye?—a dry hand?—a yellow cheek?—a white beard?—a decreasing leg? —an encreasing belly? &c. &c. &c."——I believe by a *moist eye* is not there meant, that sparkling fluid which lends an appearance of penetration, and which gives point and expression.

But I am contented to want these requisites he says I have not, as long as I am thought to possess those he allows me ——But the London Rider should not decide so pointedly that I had better stay where I am—he has not seen many characters in which I succeed better than in those four he did see.

I have played, Doctor, since I have been upon the stage, which you know is only
four

four years, upwards of *seventy* characters, and moſt of them of the firſt importance, both for character and magnitude.——Judge if my faculties have not been pretty well ſtretched, and judge if I have not a claim to ſome indulgence on that ſcore——I know you will be apt to ſay, it were better to have matured half a dozen, than to have run through ſuch a number in the crude and haſty manner I muſt neceſſarily have done ;——to which I anſwer, that this was not in my power. The people here will have variety, and our company is ſo limited, that the leaders in it are obliged to furniſh out that variety from themſelves ; nor do I believe, that in the end it will hurt me. I wiſh Mr. Woodfall had choſen any other name to pay me his compliments in, than that of THE LONDON RIDER.

To

To ufe the language of Piftol,

          " Shall pack-horfes,
" And hollow-pamper'd jades of Afia,
" Which cannot go but thirty miles a day,
" Compare with Cæfars, and with cannibals,
" And Trojan Greeks ?"

I fincerely hope, my dear friend, that your happinefs is fecure, that Mrs. D—— and all your family are in health, and that they will continue fo, as I am really interefted in every thing that concerns you. Let me hear from you, and believe me truly,

Your's, &c.

J. HENDERSON.

The

The idea of playing at London was now at an end, except some fortunate accident should give him an introduction; and this accident happened when it was least expected.

Mr. Colman having, in 1777, purchased from Mr. Foote the Patent of the Haymarket Theatre, engaged Henderson as a performer, upon terms which will appear by the following letter.

To

To Mr. I——.

January 8, 1777.

Dear I——,

I HAVE agreed with Colman, and shall
be at the Haymarket in the summer.

I am to play only my best characters,
and I am to have an hundred pounds;
besides, Colman has promised me his interest with the Chamberlain, to procure me
a benefit after his patent closes, which, if
I can compass, will be a very great thing
for me; but I depend not upon that. I
shall play Shylock first, I believe, but there
is time enough to determine that—You
can't conceive how I am in favour here—I

was

was at a masquerade last week, and got great credit.

Oh, Garrick and I are almost reconciled; he has recommended me to Drury-lane. You may almost be sure of my being at one of the theatres in London, when my time is out here. I do not yet repent my con-duct, nor have I reason; but more here-after.

My love to all your *familé.*

Your's, sincerely,

J. H.

To

To Mr. I———.

Bath, Feb. 12, 1777.

My Dear I———,

I HAVE juft had my benefit, very brilliant, very crouded, and the beft I have ever made in this place. I played Leon. I agree very much with you about Shylock; I will not make my firft appearance in it, if I can prevail with Colman to alter his opinion, and I fhall write to him for that purpofe. However, it is proper that you fhould know what that opinion was, and how it was grounded. He fays, my manner of playing it is different enough from Macklin's to excite enquiry and examination, and he payed me the compliment to add, that he thought me fufficiently grounded in the author to juftify fuch deviations, or dif-

ferences,

ferences, as there was from Macklin. He added alſo, that to make people talk and argue, and diſpute, was what he aimed at, and ſeemed to be certain, that if he could do that, my reputation would be eſtabliſhed by it. Now, though this is plauſible and flattering to me, I think with you, that the popular ſpirit is too ſtrong to be conteſted with at preſent, and therefore I propoſe, in my own mind, to begin more humbly, and riſe, if I can, by degrees. I have made a figure lately in Valentine, in Love for Love, and Oakley in the Jealous Wife, and Leon. I will play as little tragedy as poſſible in the ſummer, for more reaſons than one. The chief is, that I do not think myſelf ripe enough in the high tragic line; and another reaſon is, that tragedy will never be fol- lowed in the dog-days, except ſome extraor- dinary planet of attraction appears; and if I am neglected, I am ruined. I will play

Hamlet,

Hamlet, and *Richard the Third,* and *Shy-lock,* and perhaps *John.*

I am now ftudying Henry the Fifth, which, if I can make anfwerable to my prefent ideas of it, I may perhaps add to them, and I think no more. I fhall have infinite variety and fcope in comedy, fuch as *Falftaff, Bays, Don John, Benedick, Leon, Oakley, Valentine, Felix,* &c. &c.

Richard the Second was once revived, but the town would not bear it; there are no women in it, and the whole play demands the fineft acting to make it pleafing. By the next poft I fhall take up the hundred pound note I gave your brother H——. Have not I been a good œconomift, and I have paid near fifty pounds to J——n.

O.

I am

I am happy to hear so well of Mortimer; I do love that varlet; I hope he will continue as true to his own genius as that will be to him. I hope too, that Gainsborough will let you have my head—don't you think it a very fine likeness.

My mother desires her best wishes may be added to mine, for Mrs. I—— and yourself. She is quite recovered:—Did I tell you, we have changed our lodgings, and provide for ourselves, and I market, and purchase the tails of rabbits, and the beards of oysters, and the heads and gizzards of geese, for we leave their bodies to the mighty ones of the earth, and I buy beef steaks by the ounce, and have learnt to cut up a shrimp most dextrously. In short, we live upon the extremities of animals. I hear the butcher's boy knock at the door with as fine a sheep's tail in a tray as ever you saw in your life—it is to be roasted, and if you

were

were here, you should have two joints out of the five.

Adieu, we are very happy, and very truly am I your friend, &c.

J. HENDERSON.

In

In confequence of Mr. Colman's engagement, he came to London, and on the 11th of June 1777, begun his theatrical career in the capital with the character of Shylock, which, notwithftanding his own and his friends objections, was the part the manager introduced him in; and the manner he perfonated the ferocious Jew, fully fatisfied the propriety of Mr. Colman's choice.

I have been told, that previous to Mr. Macklin's performance of Shylock, it was looked upon as a part of little importance, and played with the buffoonery of a Jew pedlar; to the underftanding of that venerable performer, we are obliged for the firft true reprefentation of the character; but his warmeft admirers will, I think, acknowledge, that though much fterling is left, he fcarce acquired the reputation he enjoys in the Jew, from his manner of now playing
it.

it. I know it will be deemed dramatic herefy, but yet dare avow, that *I think*, except in the fenate fcene, Henderfon performed it better than *I* ever faw Mr. Macklin. In that fcene, the judicious conception of this patriarch of the theatre, fecures him from every competitor. He praifed the young adventurer with great liberality for his *fpirited* performance; and, on Henderfon's afferting, he had never had the advantage of feeing him in the character, replied, " Sir, it was not neceffary to tell *me* that; I knew you had not, or you would have played it very differently."

Teftimonials from authors to authors, were, in the laft age, deemed neceffary embellifhments to books, and as conftantly fubjoined as the *livelie pourtraiture of the painfulle writer*. Teftimonials from players to players, are not, I believe very frequent.

O 3　　　　　　　　The

The following is the only one I ever heard Henderſon ſpeak of having received; and, as I know he eſteemed approbation from a gentleman of Mr. Digges' learning, experience, and judgment, as giving a ſanction to his performance, I publiſh it as a dramatic curioſity.

To

To Mr. HENDERSON.

Friday, twelve o'clock.

DEAR SIR,

I DID myself the pleasure of waiting on you this morning, to thank you for the uncommon delight I received in seeing your excellent performance of Shakespeare's Jew —I never saw a character more justly conceived, or more happily personated—I congratulate you on the great reputation you have established : a reputation you will rather augment than diminish—I think it a thousand pities you should be doomed to a provincial banishment, when you will be so much wished for in the capital. Permit

me

me to assure you, no person is more sensible of your merit, or will rejoice more in seeing that merit rewarded, than,

Dear Sir,

Your most obedient,

And most humble servant,

WEST DIGGES.

He afterwards performed Hamlet, Leon, Falſtaff, Richard, Don John, and Bayes. He was requeſted to play *Bays*, with imitations of the different actors, which, to the credit of his prudence, he re-fuſed.

During the very hot ſummer of 1777, the Haymarket Theatre was crouded. Mr. Henderſon being announced, operated as a charm : it attracted people of the firſt rank and taſte to a play-houſe in the dog-days.

Some of the diurnal critics praiſed him for merit he did not poſſeſs, but that the motive was to ſerve Mr. Colman, there appeared *a little reaſon* to ſuſpect, from the ſame conſiſtent gentlemen being

equally

equally lavish of their abuse, when he played at Drury-lane. Of this un-candid conduct he complains in the following letter.

To

To Mr. CUMBERLAND.

October 25th, 1777.

DEAR SIR,

I A M much obliged and honoured by
your intelligence refpecting the Battle of
Haftings. I am afhamed to acknowledge,
that I have not had an hour to myfelf of
that kind that is fit to confider fo important
a matter. One fhould neither be indolent
nor fatigued, when a work of ftudy is to
be contemplated. Fatigued I have been
to an extreme degree. * * * * *.

As foon as I have gone through the Roman Father, which I now have in re-
hearfal, I fhall dedicate my ftudies to the
Battle, and hope to revive the fame pleaf-

ing

ing and magical ideas which I felt when you read it in Queen-Anne-ſtreet.

I believe, my dear ſir, you will agree that I have a moſt difficult taſk to act.

The critics call out for novelty, for ſpirit, for fire, for paſſion, for every thing in ſhort that they are taught by nature, or by reading to expect, and yet they are perpetually interrupting my emulation by the hopeleſs proſpect of ever attaining what they have been accuſtomed to delight in, from Garrick, and Macklin. I have not the vanity to think myſelf equal, by many degrees, to either, but is it not hard they will not let me be what I am, nor by their good will let the people come and ſee what that is.——I have the conſolation of very good houſes indeed, or theſe gentlemen would make my theatrical life a very pain-

ful

ful one.—There are fome public prints, that even call me names. I am honoured by one writer, who perhaps never faw me out of my dramatic drefs, with the name of pragmatical puppy ; another, in infulting irony calls me a monfter of perfection. But ftill I have good houfes.—I am told my Richard is a defpicable attempt at fomething, I know not what, but ftill I have good houfes.

I am, &c.

J. HENDERSON.

Mr.

Mr. Colman having derived material advantage from his performer's popularity, displayed great generosity at the end of the season. His conduct went "beyond the fixed and settled rules," he gave Henderson a *free benefit*, which produced upwards of two hundred pounds. He distinguished him by every attention, and frequently invited him to his table, where Henderson's delicacy and prudence once forsook him, for in the presence of a large company he took off the manger's peculiarities to his face. I need not add that so gross an insult produced a coolness on the part of Mr. Colman.

The ensuing winter he was engaged by Mr. Sheridan to perform at Drury-Lane, at a salary of ten pounds a week, and a benefit. Before this could take place it was necessary to settle his forfeiture of three hundred pounds for the failure of his Bath articles.

articles. This, I believe, was done by Mr. Sheridan giving Palmer the liberty of exhibiting the School for Scandal, which was, I should suppose, at least an adequate compensation; added to this, it was stipulated that Henderson should perform a few nights at Bath, which he did.

He had an early contempt for *stage trick*, and one of the first times he played Hamlet at Drury-Lane, was so fully impressed with the spirit of the character, that in the closet scene, when describing the two miniatures, he whirled the king's picture from his hand. This was marked in one of the public prints as an innovation too violent for a young man. " Mr. Garrick never did it." The following night he checked his imagination, and kept possession of the picture. This was a fresh occasion for carping, and one gentleman, who I think

adopted

adopted the terrific fignature of *Scourge,* obferved, " that if right the firft night, he muft confequently be wrong the fecond," and added ; " In *our* opinion Mr. Henderfon departing from the eftablifhed cuftom of the Theatre, by fometimes neglecting to kick down the chair, on the appearance of the Ghoft, which was never omitted by the greateft actor who ever graced the ftage,* and not having always *got quit* of his hat, when he ftarts, in the firft fcene, is a violation of dramatic decorum, and deferves fevere reprehenfion from the critic. Deviations fo flight as to evade the common eye, and innovations fo trifling as to be thought unworthy of notice, have led the way

* The chair in which Mr. Garrick fat, when he played in the clofet fcene, was fomewhat different from that appropriated to the queen, the cabriole feet being tapered, and placed fo much under the feat, that it fell with a touch.

way to herefies in religion, and the *abo-lifhment* of order in civil government. Let us nip error in the bud, and not by our filence give fanction to impropriety. Being once right, let us remain fo."

A friend of Henderfon's fent a reply to this curious rhapfody, which, being fhort, I fubjoin.

Two queries addreffed to the *fevere* Scourge.—Do you confider the Dramatis Perfonæ as *Autometa?* If you do, fhould not the magnificent Mr. Cox be manager, and that ingenious mechanift, Mr. Jaques Droz, prompter to your puppets? Thefe queftions were not anfwered.

On the fecond of January, 1778, he appeared in the character of Bobadil. Very high expectations were formed from the *eclat*

P
with

with which it had been received at Bath.
But *there* it was an imitation of Woodward,
which would *here* have been deemed a bur-
lefque of that moft excellent actor. Here,
I think, he failed, and, by endeavouring to
avoid Woodward's manner, departed from
the character.

I do not think myfelf at liberty to publifh
the name of the gentleman who wrote the
following letter. I know Mr. Henderfon
very properly thought himfelf honoured by
his regards, and frequently profited by his
judicious and friendly remarks.

To

To Mr. Henderson.

Dublin, Nov. 13, 1777.

I SEE clearly, that you think I am not
awake to your abilities, and that I am rather
cold in your praife—I do affure you, you are
miftaken—I know and feel your great fupe-
riority to the prefent race of actors, and I
have had, within thefe twelve months, frequent opportunities of declaring it. Mr.
Garrick, and Mr. B. Sheridan, can teftify
for me, that I ventured to *pronounce*, (that
was the expreffion I made ufe of) before
them, and Mr. Gibbon the hiftorian, laft
winter, that you was an excellent performer
in every thing, and capital in comedy.
Thefe were my words, (which Sheridan
and Gibbon, I dare fay, thought very pe-

P 2

remptory

remptory and affuming) but I was called upon by Mr. Garrick to declare my opinion as one which he relied upon, and Mr. Garrick immediately added his own fuffrage, and told Mr. Sheridan, that it was his bufinefs to fecure you as foon as poffible—I rather dwell upon this *literal* fact, becaufe Davies, in anfwer to my affertion, that Garrick had earneftly recommended you to Sheridan, fays abfurdly, that it was after fuch recommendation was *ineffectual*, and that you was obliged to wait 'till Sheridan had his own evidence of your powers and merit.

Here Davies grofsly miftakes ; whether wilfully, or not, I am not fure, for Garrick recommended you whenever he could catch you. At the lateft, when your Bath articles fhould expire ; and even then, Sheridan, in my prefence, talked of the fcheme

of

of getting you from Palmer, and sending Grist to Bath. This Mr. Garrick and I both approved of — * * * * * * * * * * * *.

As to newspaper puffing, (which Davies is so fond of) it is the foolisheft thing in the world, because it produces all those criticisms which you allude to. As to conversation puffing from good authority, I think quite otherwise of it—The generality of the world are much led by their own circle; but newspaper commendation is universally considered as the advertisement of a quack doctor. I saw in one paper, Bensley preferred to you in Horatius. I have not seen your Horatius, but I *have* your Alcanor, and I am sure your Horatius must be good.

P 3Lucius

Lucius Junius Brutus, and the Battle of Haftings, have been promifed places in this feafon for more than a year paft—Shirley, I believe, for years.

As to the Law of Lombardy, the author thinks the parts are equal. I differ from him widely. There is a young gallant knight driven to a defpair of jealoufy, by the villainous acts of a plotting rival. They fight in the end, and are the confpicuous men; but the perfon worked upon I always think a better part than the worker. I go fo far as to think Alonzo a finer character than Zanga. Polidore muft be the favourite. He is *Pofthumus*, if poffible, more impaffioned. This being the caft, which you feemed to me to decline, I naturally looked at the other character for you. But nothing is, or can, be yet fettled about it. There is an old king, and father alfo,

that

that requires an excellent actor ; *that*, I con-
clude muſt be crucified, as the fine part of
Almada was.

As for your ſearch for new readings, I do
not like them. Your reſtoration of good
paſſages I can never diſapprove of. That
in Richard I like very well. * * * * *
* * * * * * * *.

To return to your innovations—I cannot
ſee, how changed readings, and points, are
in any ſort connected with the ſtile of
acting. It is introducing criticiſm into
acting, which I think never ſhould be ;
and if it ſhould be bad criticiſm (ſuch
as the croaking raven) what can be ſaid
for it ?

I hear

I hear your laboured shew of propriety much condemned—But all these remarks are to your honour.   They would not be made, but that you are confessedly at the head of the stage.

Your sincere

And obedient servant,

E. T.

You say all your novelties are defensible; if I thought so, I should not blame you for them—You ask me, if you have ever spoiled the sense—I think grossly in the *croaking raven*, if you speak it as my reporter informs me.

In

In the summer of 1778 he went to Ireland. His reception from that generous people, is described in the following letter.

To

To Mr. I————.

Dublin, 5th June, 1780.

No, my dear boy, I am as well as I ought
to expect, though my arms, at leaſt one
of them, are troubleſome.   The true reaſon of my not writing is, that I am half
aſhamed to tell you the conſequences of my
expedition, but I now find that I ought
not to impute it to my own weakneſs of
fame or talent, but to the univerſal diſtreſs
and poverty this kingdom at preſent labours
under.

The firſt character I played, was Hamlet,
and carried hence no more than fourteen
pound three ſhillings, though the Lord
Lieutenant did me the honour of his prefence.

fence. The next night I voluntarily and chearfully gave to a charity for the diftreffed manufacturers: it was Falftaff—not five pounds in the galleries, nor above feventy in the whole houfe; a ftrong inftance of their inability upon fo good, fo ufeful an occafion. My third character was Shylock, and there was not expences in the houfe.— This night I fhall play Richard.—I have given up all thoughts of getting any thing, except by a benefit, which I have reafon to hope will be handfome, for I cannot defcribe to you how I am careffed by the people of fafhion, the only few who can go to a play. The Duke of Leinfter does me every kindnefs imaginable. I was laft night at the Caftle, at the ball and fupper. More than a hundred people of rank and fafhion, and tafte, defired to be made known to me.—In fhort, more flattery, more attention, and confequently more happinefs,

I never

I never tafted—my fpirits have been in one ftate of the moft delicious delirium ever fince I touched this fhore.—I have no time though, for it is the cuftom here to wait upon ftrangers, and my lodgings are crouded when I am at home.—Except lodgings it has not coft me a fhilling fince I came to this place, nor would it if I were to ftay here this fix months.—I am very glad I came, becaufe it will extend my connections and my fame, though it may not be very advantageous to my purfe.   I intended to have written a whimfical account of my voyage; we were forty hours upon the water, but I was not fick above two hours the whole time, and that moderately.——I don't know what my friend E—— has done for me, nor when I am to quit this place.   Whenever I do, it will be with reluctance—but if it will not take up too much of his time, I fhould like to know about it.

Mrs.

Mrs. Barry is here, but she finds the condition of the people, and I believe will not play, if she does I will make safe conditions for myself. I am to have ten guineas a night, and if the house amounts to a fixed sum, fifteen. But my benefit is my only object.

J. H.

Thanks for the Plays.

After

After his return from Ireland, on the 13th of January 1779, the writer of thefe anec-dotes had the honour of prefenting to him, that beft of all good gifts a wife, * and the following year, as fponfor, gave the name of Harriet to a daughter, who, by the death of her father, has loft not only a protector, but an inftructor very capable of forming and improving her mind,

Among other characters new to him in the metropolis, he performed King John.

One of his friends wrote him a few remarks, which I have fubjoined, as I think there are fome fenfible ftrictures upon his playing.——The advice at the conclufion,

that

* She was daughter to Mr. Figgins, of Chippenham in Somerfetfhire.

that " when preparing for a new part he should retire to his own room, &c." was founded upon the writer's having obferved Mr. *Henderfon's mode of preparation,* which was almoft invariably this. When a new part was appointed him, he firft read the play : I mention this, becaufe I have heard the practice is not univerfal among the dramatis perfonæ. He then imprinted the words of the character he was to perfonate upon his memory, which, to him, was not a very difficult tafk; looked over the play flightly a fecond time, and then laid it afide, and though this ceremony was frequently gone through a fortnight before the performance, feldom looked at it again.—The evening before his appearance, was ufually preceded by a hearty dinner, a chearful, but moderate glafs of wine, and a game at cribbage, which

was

was almoſt always his amuſement until a few minutes before the curtain drew up, and he was obliged, ſometimes very unwilling, to appear at the Theatre.

To

To Mr. Henderson.

Dear Henderson,

I LAST night sat by Kenrick during the play, in the front boxes—I had a good deal of conversation with him—He seemed not unwilling to do justice to your merit, but complained of your method of toning your voice; by copying Garrick's under-play, he said you were scarce intelligible to the audience—I assured him that he was greatly mistaken, for that you had not very often seen Garrick, nor could you copy his King John, which Garrick had not acted for thirty years past. However, he was so far right that you apparently wanted spirit, and your voice was lower and more indistinct than the crack'd pipkin of the king

of

of France.—You loft opportunities of getting applaufe with Pandolph, you gave little or no force to the popular, as well as juft fentiments of an Englifh king, difdaining to be governed by an Italian prieft—Your action was extremely confined and fpiritlefs—your general idea of the rafcal John, who compared to Richard is as a foot-pad, or pick-pocket, oppofed to a highwayman, was juft; your fcene with Hubert · was well planned, and mafterly, though you was rather too low—I never loft a word of your's 'till laft night—Kenrick obferved that you wanted variety—In the dying fcene, you made ample amends for all deficiencies in the foregoing acts—Kenrick owned you was excellent.

And now let me remind you, of your neglecting to give due fire and fpirit to that

excellent

excellent fcene of John with Hubert in the fourth act—your reproaches loft all effect with the audience from under-play, or taking your voice too low. You fuffered Hubert to make the moft of that paffionate interview, and to rob you of the applaufe you would have merited by a proper exertion of your powers.—I told K———— that I fancied you was not well, or at leaft not in fpirits.

Believe me I do not aim to teach or direct you, who know fo much more of the matter than I can pretend to, but the lefs fkilful ftander-by can fee defects in a very able gamefter.

I would recommend your imitation of Garrick in one part of his conduct : whenever he had a new or capital character to act, he faw no company that day, and dined

alone

alone upon a trifling diſh. This was his conſtant practice, I believe from his firſt treading the ſtage 'till he left it.

On ſuch an occaſion as acting a new part, &c. I would after dining with Mr. and Mrs. I——, retire to my own room, nor would I be diſturbed by any viſitor whatſoever.—— I tell you again and again, you will deſtroy both voice and ſtomach by your curſed hot ſippings—excuſe my freedom,

Yours, ever,

T. D.

Saturday eleven o'Clock.

The fat parſon G——— is juſt gone paſt to preach a charity ſermon.

In

In confequence of this letter and fome other advice, he once changed his cuftom, retired to his chamber and ftudied his part on the day of playing. The confequence was a coldly correct, and moft vapid perform- ance, which convinced him and his friends that his firft practice was right, at leaft for him.—He ferioufly vowed no earthly power fhould induce him to repeat the experi- ment, adding, at the fame time, that he thought it poffible, that a number of very grave men, who muzzed away much time alone in their own apartments, were quite as likely to be fleeping as ftudying.

During the time he performed at Drury-Lane, Mr. Sheridan the elder, very properly confidering his peculiar excellence in fpeak-ing tales, fables, or any light airy compofi-tion, revived Sir John Vanbrugh's Æfop, with fome alterations, which, from having heard

Q 3

Henderfon

Henderſon read it, I think he would have made a moſt popular and entertaining character. He entered with true humour into the ſpirit of the little tales, and gave full force to the *Cervantic* gravity of the old moraliſt. But the town were too faſtidious to ſuffer the performance in even its altered ſtate, Mr. Yates perſonated a country ſquire, a character the preſent age know only from deſcription ; the ſavage preferred his hounds to his wife, and Æſop was driven from the ſtage,

Among thoſe who moſt violently inſiſted upon its being withdrawn, were ſome of the critical leaders of the taſte of the town, who conſidered, and perhaps with good reaſon, that ſhould it ſucceed, the fabuliſt might be made a vehicle to anſwer the diurnal remarks which ornament our

daily

daily papers, and therefore very prudently filenced him the firſt night.

In the ſummer of 1779 he returned to Dublin, and was gratified by every mark of attention, noticed by people of diſtinction, and received, not merely as an actor, but a companion, by families of the firſt conſequence.

The annexed letter is one example, among many others, of the reſpect with which the gentlemen of Ireland, diſtinguiſh and protect genius, in any ſituation.

Mr. Gardiner's teſtimony is ſo high an honour to Henderſon's memory, that I ſhould not be juſtified in withholding it. I hope,—I believe,—the ſame liberality of ſentiment which dictated ſuch a letter, will pardon its inſertion.

Q 4

Copy

*Copy of a Letter from Mr. Gardiner to Lord
Doneraile.*

Black-Rock, *July* 6th, 1779.

MY DEAR LORD,

A S Mr. Henderson is going to Cork,
to perform there, I thought I could not
do him a greater service than to recommend him to your attention. He has given
us much entertainment here, and I doubt not
will afford you equal pleasure in the line of
his profession. I have had frequent opportunities of being in company with him and
Mrs. H. and have found them so agreeable,
that I need make no apology for introducing them to your lordship's acquaintance,
particularly,

particularly, as such talents as his, united with good humour, and good breeding,
are at this day peculiarly rare.

I remain, &c.

J. GARDINER.

The

The enſuing ſeaſon Mr. Sheridan and Henderſon diſagreed upon terms, the expectations of the latter being higher than the manager thought proper to comply with; what thoſe expectations were founded upon, are deſcribed as follows.

To

To Mr. I———.

Dublin, June 29, 1779.

I WAITED for fomething of more importance than our fafe arrival to inform you
of, and now I have a fubject. The principal people are fo defirous of my wintering
here, that they have made me the moft flattering, the moft honourable propofals. To
fecure me from the *accidents* (ACCIDENT
is here a word of great pith and moment,
and ufed for fafety, becaufe letters may be
miflaid) which may happen in a negotiation
with the Irifh manager; they will raife a
fubfcription among themfelves, and the Lord
Lieutenant himfelf offers a hundred guineas
towards it; the reft will amount to a larger
fum than I fhould receive in England, even
if my demands were complied with, and I

confider

consider the house in Buckingham-street as untenanted, and pay the rent myself. Now I am in a state of most tormenting suspense; for I hear nothing either from the elder, or the younger Sheridan—They seem to have no great earnestness in their wish that I should continue with them, and yet I do not care to stay here, unless they positively answer me, *yes* or *no.*

This place is poor beyond all names of poverty, at least so the people say, and I am sure the Theatre bears the marks of it; but if I stay, I depend upon those who can-not be poor in any country. Mrs. Crawford certainly stays here, and I shall have the ad-vantage of playing with her. C———d is abominated by the critics, and all people here are critics. I am now going to Corke, so that you must direct to me there. If you would see the elder Mr. Sheridan, and

learn

learn from him what I am to do, I fhould be glad. I dare not fend him the propofals that are made me at large, left it fhould be conftrued an artifice to raife my confequence in England, or a treachery to the proprietors here. But fomething I muft do, and fpeedily.

Whether the propofals here are accepted or not, nothing can be more favourable to my reputation, than their having been made by people of fuch rank, and tafte, and importance, as they are.

Adieu, my deareft friend,

Affure yourfelf, I am moft affectionately,

Your's, &c.

J. HENDERSON.

July 16, 1779.

THE very day that I wrote to you, I wrote alfo to the elder Sheridan ; I told him my offers, and gave him 'till the firft of Auguft to determine. I fhall not recede from my claims, as I think them juft.

I yefterday received a letter from the treafurer of Drury-lane, acquainting me, that he was ordered by the proprietors, ten days before, to write to me, and to inform me that they were ready to treat with me upon the fame terms as laft year. I have no doubt that this was written in confequence of mine to S————, and that *the ten days* is a lye. This letter I anfwered, by faying, that Mr. Sheridan, the elder, was ac-

quainted

quainted with my refolutions, and that I
fhould be governed by his anfwer, which I
fhall, and by the firft of Auguft I fhall
decide. Nothing is more likely, than that
S—— would wifh to be the hero: he probably wifhes it, and it may probably happen.
I do not fee, my dear lad, what you can
do; I muft wait his reply, and act accord-
ingly. At all events, it is an honourable
retreat for me, and I may be more wanted
another year. I muft write more at large,
when I know more, and have more time.

J. H.

To Mr. I————.

Cork, Aug. 24, 1779.

DEAR JACK,

MY letter to E———— ftates all my defighs, and I need not repeat them to you. When you have read the letter will you fend it? I write to E————, becaufe I would have it fhewn to Sheridan; and I am refolved to adhere to my terms. I can make a very handfome bargain here, and complete it in three months. I fhall get more money, and be lefs a flave, and efcape the unworthy treatment I have found in London. I feel my own importance more than ever I did, and I will not be trampled on. Pray, my dear boy, copy, or get this letter copied, for I have not time, and learn, if you

can,

can what anſwer he gets, and write to me at Birmingham. I do not urge *him* to an anſwer, becauſe it looks like too much anxiety.

J. H.

To

To Mr. E———.

Aug. 24, 1779.

DEAR E———,

YOU will, perhaps, be difappointed when I decline Mr. Sheridan's offer, but you ought, of all people, to be the leaft fo, becaufe you muft remember the converfation you was prefent at, between Mr. S——— and myfelf, when I made my firft agreement with him. You remember, that my falary was no more than ten pounds a week, be-caufe my forfeiture was urged, and you re-member Mr. Sheridan urged that forfeiture being *equally* paid, whether in *money*, or in *property*. You remember alfo, that Mr. Sheridan urged, that I fhould be moderate in my firft claims, and *rife*, by degrees, in the Theatre, and now he propofes that I

fhould

fhould fink in it; for fifteen guineas a week is not more than I had, computing my for-feiture, and I ought in juftice to have ranked in the Theatre agreeable to *that* falary, though, in the quietnefs of my difpofition, I forbore a claim which might be troublefome without material advantage. My reception in this kingdom, among fuch perfons as it is moft an actor's honour as well as intereft to pleafe, has not moderated my opinion of the juftice of my claim, to an equal falary, and equal rank, with Mr. Smith. When I converfed with the elder Mr. Sheridan in the Park, he told me, that Mr. S——, his fon, could not deny the reafonablenefs of my claim, but that, for certain reafons, it could not be complied with for the next feafon; that if I would ftay on my prefent falary for one year more, I fhould have my demands in future. To this I anfwered, agreeable to my defire of accommodation, &c.

that

that if he would give me twelve guineas per week *now*, and fifteen guineas a week in a future season, I would be content. If Mr. Sheridan had made me *that* offer now, I believe I should have closed with him, but I cannot accept his twelve pounds, and no assurance of rising the next season. I could have contented myself with postponing my claim, but am not content to relinquish it.

I have received a letter from Mr. T. S. in which he tells me, that the patentees are determined to raise no salaries, and yet I am assured, that an actor, with whom it would do me no very great honour to be compared, has obtained an encrease of his. I know very well, how little force, arguments and reasons have with managers, and, therefore, I do not use them there; but this is, my friend, to justify myself to you—Whilst I

feel

feel no diminution of my own powers, nor any decline of the public approbation, I see no reason why I should humble myself to the disadvantage of my interest, or my importance in a Theatre.—My design, therefore, is to set off for England, play a few nights at Birmingham, proceed to London; from thence return to Ireland about December, which will be time enough to compleat entirely the plan I have in meditation, and to answer all my designs. I shall be in Buckingham-street, I hope, by the latter end of September, unless I find it convenient to perform longer in the country. I hope you will not condemn me for not accepting Mr. Sheridan's offer, nor think I am at all in exile. Why should I leave a place where I am caressed by all ranks of people, to accept terms that degrade me from my first conditions, and keep me inferior to those whom the public do not prefer to me.—I

must

muſt remind you, that the conditions on which I ſtay here, are ſuch as, I believe, have not happened to any other actor, and, therefore, muſt do me honour in the world. I may, poſſibly, paſs my next ſummer in London to great advantage, as well as convenience; in the mean time, I will not weakly embrace the fetters which the London coalition are forging for us. It requires no very great foreſight to obſerve the toils which are gathering round us. I thank God, I need not at this period ruſh into them, and, therefore, I feel eaſier than when I left England.

I am, &c.

J. H.

P. S. In order that my terms may be fully underſtood, I repeat to you, that I ſhould

ſo

ſo far compromiſe the matter, to accept
of twelve guineas for the next ſeaſon,
and fifteen for the two ſucceeding—But
I cannot play for twelve, without an aſ-
ſurance of the reſt.

At

At the commencement of the winter 1779, he removed to Covent Garden, at a falary of twelve pounds a week, and performed feveral characters, new to him, with encreafed reputation — Macbeth, for the firft time at this Theatre, on the 18th of October.

When he appeared with the daggers after the murder of Duncan, I think the countenance of horror and remorfe which he affumed, was equal to any exhibition I ever faw upon the ftage, and much critical knowledge of the character was difplayed through the whole; yet in the other fcenes he wanted the fpeaking terrors of Mr. Garrick's look and action, which can no more be defcribed than they can be equalled.

The fummer of 1780 he paffed at Liver-pool. To fay he was well received, will

be

be a repetition of that which has been already said, but, furely, the actor who has powers cf attraction fufficient to induce men of fcience to come from diftant parts of a province to be prefent at his performance, muft be allowed to derive fome honour from their attendance; efpecially when it is confidered, that province was Lanca-fhire; for it will not be eafy to find any country fo eminently diftinguifhed for tho liberality and fcientific knowledge, of thofe who have been, and are its inha-bitants.

In the winter he returned to Covent-Garden. Among other characters he performed Wolfcy. His fenfible fpeaking and accurate elocution marked the character, but in fome of the fcenes he wanted that dignity

which

which the poet and hiftorian * (for an hiftorian our immortal dramatift may be called)
has given to the haughty Cardinal.

He played Sir John Brute, and I thought
pleafantly, but Mr. Garrick obferved, " it
was the city Sir John, for egad he had neither the air nor the manner of the rake of
fafhion."

I believe it was in this feafon he firft perfonated Iago, a character in which perhaps he has not been equalled. A very
good idea of the manner in which he

looked

* A writer of fome eminence fays, that the great
Duke of Marlborough was ignorant of Englifh hiftory,
and to prove his affertion, gives an inftance of his Grace
having once quoted Shakefpeare, as an authority upon
a difputed point. The inftance was furely unfortunate.

looked it, may be formed from Bartolozzi's engraving; when I add it was from a fketch by Stuart, *though at only one fitting,* 'tis fcarce neceffary to fay it exhibits a moft ftriking refemblance.

Sir Charles Eafy he played for a be-nefit. The character fat heavy upon him. I remember Foote ufed to tell of an eminent actor of the old fchool, who being informed he muft play Richard the Third, the following night, returned for anfwer to the manager, " that his rheumatifm was fo bad he could fcarcely ftir hand or foot, but if they would get up the Carelefs Huf-band, he was ready to play *Sir Charles Eafy,* inftead of the king."

Finding it impoffible to make his own terms in the fummer of 1781, he had not any Theatrical employment, except that he

one night played Falſtaff at the Haymarket, for the benefit of Mr. Edwin.

His hours of leiſure he frequently employed in copying old plays, and I verily
believe it was upon theſe occaſions only,
that he read them, for no man had leſs
reverence for the BLACK LETTER than
Mr. John Henderſon. His opinion of
large libraries was not much more favourable. He uſed to quote the remark
of ſomebody, who ſaid, " that moſt
men who got together vaſt quantities of
books, put him in mind of the Italian
ſinger who founded a Seraglio." I believe,
in general, the greateſt collectors are not
the moſt remarkable for being the deepeſt
readers. Indeed the time taken up in hunt-
ing after *ſcarce books*, does not leave much
learned leiſure for peruſing them.

The

In the fummer of 1782 he played at Liverpool, where I think his benefit amounted to nearly two hundred pounds.

In the winter he performed Lufignan, but his powers were unequal to either that or Lear. The pathetic was not his *forte*, had he been left to the choice of his own characters, I believe he would no more have played Lear than Romeo. He thought highly, and not unjuftly of his own merit in fpeaking the Choruffes to Henry the Fifth, which being rather an unpopular play, he did not, I believe, appear in after January 1779, when I faw him. His figure acquired grace from the Vandyke habit. His recitation led me to regret it was not repeated. He was accurate, animated, energetic.

In

In the November of 1783 he appeared in Tamerlane, to Mr. Kemble's Bajazet; but the fire of the tyrannic Bajazet predominated over the tame Tamerlane, who, notwithstanding the avowed intention of the poet, was to give a semblance of, and pay a compliment to, our third William, is a vapid, heavy, and insipid part.

The summer of 1784 he passed at Edinburgh, and it was observed, that the *Reverendi*, and *Reverendissimi*, laid aside their ancient prejudices*, and appeared in a playhouse, to behold Mrs. Siddons, and Mr. Henderson.

* These prejudices were not peculiar to Scotland; the same narrowness of sentiment pervaded a numerous class of people in this kingdom, not very many years ago. On a set of itinerants being once tolerably well received at Kidderminster, in Worcestershire, a Mr. Watson nailed a card, with the following lines, upon

the

Henderſon. How different were the ſentiments of this people in the days of that ſevere ſcourge of diſſipation, John Knox, when the repreſentation of a play would have excited horror, and the whole company had been devoted to deſtruction, as a regiment under the banner of the woman of Babylon.

During

the door of the barn where they enacted, which was dignified with the name of, *The Summer Royal Theatre.*

    " How art thou fallen, oh! Kidderminſter;
    " When every ſpulſter, ſpinner, ſpinſter,
    " Whoſe fathers liv'd in † Baxter's prayers,
    " Are now run gadding after players:
    " Oh! Richard, couldſt thou take a ſurvey,
    " Of this vile place, for ſin ſo ſcurvy,
    " Thy pious ſhade, enrag'd would ſcold them,
    " And make the barn too hot to hold them."

† Richard Baxter, who was very many years miniſter of that p'ace.

During the summer of 1785, he performed a few nights at Dublin, and was honoured by an invitation to the Caſtle, where he read the ſtory of Le Fevre, and ſome other ſelect paſſages, from his favourite Sterne, to the Duke and Dutcheſs of Rutland, and their court.

In the Lent ſeaſon, Mr. Sheridan and he united in public readings at Freemaſons Hall. The terms were thought high, but juſtified by ſucceſs. The opinion entertained of them by the public, may be gathered from the crouds who attended every night during their continuance, and from the ſum which was gained; I think not leſs than eight hundred pounds. Having in a former page given my opinion of his performance, I need not repeat it. He however read into reputation ſome things which

ſeemed

feemed to have been gathered to the dull of ancient days, and but for fuch a revival had probably been ftill covered with the cloak of oblivion.*   Had Mr. Henderfon lived, this entertainment would have been continued, as he requefted from a gentleman eminent for his tafte and judgement,† a felection from thofe writers moft likely to be popular.

Previous to his voyage to Dublin, fome little differences between Mr. Harris and him had been accommodated, and he renewed an engagement for four years, I have been told, at feventeen, eighteen, nineteen and

S   twenty

---

* *One* Printfeller fold 6000 copies of John Gilpin's Race, which had been feveral years before printed in one of the public papers, but fcarcely noticed.

† Mr. Caleb Whitefoord.

twenty pounds a week. But his laft performance was Horatius in the Roman Father, on the third of November, 1785.

He was foon after feized with a diforder which feemed to have fubmitted to medicine, but when his complaints put on the moft favourable appearance, a fudden death deprived the public of an excellent performer, and his friends of an agreeable companion, on the 25th of November, 1785, in the 40th year of his age.

An eminent furgeon gives the following account :

" Henderfon's liver was entirely undifeafed ; the lungs in perfect health ; the brain had no extravafation, whatever to external appearance. His ftomach was preternaturally ftrong. His heart was the only

part

part of the fyftem which failed. His heart was literally broken, that is, it had loft its accuftomed firmnefs of tone. It is by far the ftouteft mufcle in the human body, and the leading veffels were all offified, or offifying. In fhort, if I had not known Mr. Henderfon, and feen his face, his teeth, and his hair, I fhould have fuppofed from his heart, that his age had been ninety."

On the third of December following, he was interred in Weftminfter Abbey, near Doctor Johnfon and Mr. Garrick, the chapter and the choir attending to pay refpect to his memory. His pall was fupported by the honourable Mr. Byng, Mr. Malone, Mr. Whitefoord, Mr. Stevens, and Mr. Hoole.

S 2

I have

I have not feen any epitaph to his memory, nor is it eafy to write one properly defcriptive of his profeffion.

" The ACTOR only, fhrinks from time's award;
Feeble tradition is HIS memory's guard;
By whofe faint breath his merits muft abide,
Unvouch'd by proof—to fubftance unallied !"

The moft concife Epitaph I recollect to
have feen upon a player, was

EXIT BURBAGE.

From the time of his *entré* on a London ftage, he was overwhelmed with indifcriminate and ill judged flattery. This
might ferve the manager, but injured the
player, and inflated the man.

It fo far kindled the embers of vanity in
his mind, as to demand the full exercife of

his

his underſtanding to keep them from a blaze. It called forth critical oppoſition, which ſometimes produced too ſevere a ſcrutiny.

His death has embalmed his name, ſince that time we have had, not characters, but echoing plaudits. Profeſſing to deſcribe what Henderſon was, they tell you what a player and a man ought to be.

Such eulogies diſplay the ingenuity of the writer, but do not much ſanctify the object of their adulation.

They have enveloped his character in the miſt of panegyric, and in their zeal to con-ſecrate his memory have forgotten that ex-ceſs of decoration diſguiſes and deſtroys the reſemblance, of thoſe it is intended to dig-

S 3

nify;

nify; for to all the defcriptions of him which I have feen, it was neceffary to in-fcribe the name, or I fhould never have fufpected fuch high coloured pictures were intended as portraits of Henderfon.

Abfolute perfection is not the lot of humanity, and after all the fine things which have been faid, his relative merit is the criterion by which he muft be tried, nor will that merit fuffer much diminution by being oppofed to thofe with whom he was cotemporary.

If it fhould be thought I am too minute, I can only anfwer, that when reading of a man who was eminent, I have ever wifhed to know what were his peculiar difpofitions, and domeftic habits, by what qualities he attracted attention, and what were the methods by which he acquired reputation.

By

By some it may be thought that I over-
rate his abilities, and there may be those
who will think I have not allowed him all
that he possessed.   In the delineation of a
man's person, or disposition, I consider likeness to the original as the leading excellence,
and that I have attempted in the following

C H A R A C T E R.

As an actor he had many disadvantages
to cope with.   His height was below the
common standard.   He had an uncompacted
frame.   His limbs were ill proportioned;
they were too short; he had not much of
that flexibility of countenance which anti-
cipates the tongue, that language of the
eye which prepares the spectator for the

                coming

coming fentence, enchains attention, and en-
fures partiality. *

His voice wanted the melifluous filver
found which charms the ear, and was deficient in that dignified ftrength which commands refpect. It was not fuited to the
foftnefs of love, where the very found produces fympathy, nor to the wild rage of
tyranny, which awes the multitude.

But the ftrength of his judgment, and
the fervency of his mind, broke through
the mounds which nature feemed to have
placed between him and excellence.

His

---

* He frequently faid, " Whenever he threw meaning
into his eye, *it was from fomewhat which lay behind it,*
for he was confcious, *naturally,* it was heavy, and deftitute of expreffion." In the hours when his countenance was lighted up, it bore a ftrong refemblance to
a portrait of Betterton, by Sir Godfrey Kneller, in the
poffeffion of Mr. Samuel Ireland.

His comprehenfion was ample, his knowledge diverfified, and his elocution accurate.

Where fenfible recitation was the leading feature of a character, he had no fuperior. In the varieties of Shakefpeare's foliloquy, where more is meant than meets the ear, he had no equal.

In that fpecies of eloquence, he difcriminated with peculiar propriety the melancholy Jacques, and the penfive Hamlet, the whimfical Benedick, and the voluptuous Falftaff. In the whole of that part he was without a competitor, and not having left any lawful fucceffor, the humour of the fat knight muft be confined to the clofet.

Being little acquainted with fencing, or dancing, his deportment was neither eafy

nor

nor difengaged, and in fcenes where the former accomplifhment was neceffary, appeared to great difadvantage. Sometimes the fuperior fkill of his opponent ftruck the fword from his hand, at the moment which required its firmeft grafp—yet the character of Hamlet, he fuftained with fuch tafte, feeling, and propriety, that we forgot every light imperfection; and, except when he would faw the air with rather too much famenefs, he approached very near perfection. His manner of fpeaking three words, " *The fair Ophelia!*" ftill vibrates upon my ear. It was equal to Mrs. Crawford's, *was he alive?* Superior it could not be.

In the inftructions to the players, it will not be violating truth, to fay, he excelled Mr. Garrick. In one, we faw the Manager; in the other, the Prince of Denmark.

His

His range was extensive, especially in comedy. I do not so much mean in the number of parts, as their opposition of character*.

In the flimsy declamation of modern tragedy, he added little to his reputation. Shakespeare was the deity he worshipped, entered into the spirit of the characters, as drawn by that mighty master of the human heart, and feeling with enthusiasm, exhibited them with ardour. Yet to some he was unequal; and who has been able to personate all the creations of a Shakespeare's boundless fancy?

He

* To instance a few. What can be more dissimilar than Iago and Benedick; Hamlet and Falstaff; Shylock and Posthumus; Jaques and Don John; Brutus and Comus; Cardinal Wolsey and Sir John Brute; Leon and Sir Giles Overreach.

He had moſt uncommon powers of imitation, and gave, with the voice and geſture,
the countenance, turn of thought, and language of the perſon whoſe manner he
aſſumed*.

Of his abilities as a writer, I have had
ſo frequent occaſion to give my opinion

in

* I recollect a circumſtance, which will more fully
explain what I mean.

When I once came with him from the late Doctor
Johnſon's, I remarked that we had forgotren to mention
one of his old friends having juſt married a third wife.
I added, " What would the Doctor have ſaid to it ?"
" Sir," replied Henderſon, " he would would have ſaid,
man is born to be deceived. We ſee daily inſtances
where expectation ſubdues experience. This will be
an additional example of the fallacy of hope, and diſap-
pointment of expectation. Yet we muſt allow the man
has *courage*, or after the ſufferings of two campaigns, he
would not voluntarily expoſe himſelf on the forlorn hope.
—*He will be blown up, Sir !*"

in this volume, that I will not repeat what has been already ſaid—I ſubmit them to the judgment of the reader.

He was a cloſe and acute reaſoner, and an expert logician. Though ignorant of the *names* of his weapons of argument, he could wield them with adroitneſs and power.

In the polite arts he had a good taſte; to an eye that quickly diſcerned defects in ſculpture, or painting, he joined a freedom of ridicule, which did not add to the number of his friends amongſt the ſecond claſs of artiſts.

His memory was uncommonly tenacious, and to that he was more indebted than to laborious ſtudy, or cloſe application, for in his early years he was indolent. But his

quickneſs

quicknefs of perception foon attained whatever he attempted, and once attained it became his own.

He ufed to expatiate on Dr. Johnfon's
tendency to fuperftition, and affected more
freedom of thinking than he poffeffed, for
he believed much which he would not acknowledge.

His fpirits were generally high, but there
were hours, even after he had the moft
flattering profpects of fame and fortune,
when they funk into the loweft depreffion.*
Whether he acquired this tendency from

the

* At fuch times he has often told me the following
ftory :—When his brother was ten, and he not more
than eight years of age, their well being depending upon
the life of their mother, fhe was afflicted with a violent

nervous

the books he read, or his difpofition led him to fuch ftudies, I will not determine; it is however certain that his reading was uncommonly

nervous diforder, which had funk her into a deep melancholy. While fuffering under this, fhe one morning left her houfe and children, who waited her return with impatience. Night approached, but their parent did not come. Full of terror, the two boys went in fearch of her. Ignorant what courfe to take, they wandered until midnight, about the places where fhe ufed to walk, but wandered without fuccefs. They agreed to return home, but neither of them knew the way. Fatigued, alarmed, diftreffed, they fat down on a bank to weep, when they obferved at fome diftance a luminous appearance, and fuppofing it a candle in fome friendly habitation, haftily directed their fteps towards it. As they moved, the light moved alfo, and glided from field to field, for a confiderable time. At length, it feemed fixed, and on their near approach, vanifhed on the fide of a large piece of water. On the margin, they found their mother in a ftate from which fhe was roufed by the prefence and tears of her children.

This

uncommonly multifarious. It comprehended all books upon apparitions, illusions of the devil, and visions, from *Adye's Candle in the Dark* to *Calif's Wonders of the invisible World*. He had trod the whole circle of witchcraft, from *the History of the Witch of Endor, to the Story of Mary Squires*. Books of horror he had perused from *Fox's Martyrology, to the Account of the Dutch Cruelties at Amboyna*. To all this he added a thorough knowledge of the English classics, whose beauties he fully conceived, and eminently displayed, by the judgment, variety, and humour of his public readings. He knew the French language

This he has often asserted, he religiously believed to be neither an *ignus fatuus*, nor a creation of the imagination, but a kind interposition of Providence, for the preservation of the widow, and the widow's sons.

guage well, and fpoke it with great fluency and elegance.

His temper was placid, and under very uncommon government; I have not the recollection of ever having feen him in a paffion. He was not afhamed of obligations, but frequent in his acknowledgments.

In the acquirement of friends he was fortunate. The later years of his life were honoured with the notice of men from whofe converfation much was to be gathered, and his own equability of temper, and accomodating manners conciliated their regards.

If there was fometimes a little interchange of flattery, it was perhaps equally gratifying to each party. Henderfon faid, " it is the commerce of life, and when any one avows himfelf fo faftidious that

T   his

his mind revolts at such incense, we may fairly presume, he pretends to reject what was never offered, and rails at that branch of devotion, because he is not the object of it." He acknowledged it pleased him, and boldly asserted that no actor could perform well unless he was flattered, both in and out of the theatre. *

Like

* I think it was the late Mr. Topham Beauclerc, who inserted as a note in Cibber's Apology—That Mr. Garrick told him, when he read Lethe to his Majesty, he felt such a pressure upon his spirits, as disabled him from giving any force to the different characters of his own farce. His powers were frozen, and he was scarce capable of reading it to the conclusion. "Conceive to yourself, said he, a man wrapped up in a wet blanket reading a play to a king, and you will have a perfect idea of my situation."

This proves what Cibber asserts in his Apology, vol. 2. page 76. That *actors accustomed to loud and general plaudits cannot exert themselves without.*

Like his predeceſſor in his moſt popular character, he was not averſe to the pleaſures of a good table, and they were well beſtowed upon him; he became exhilarated. I never ſaw him play Falſtaff with ſo much glee, as one evening of a lord-mayor's day, when he had dined and drank ſack and ſugar at the houſe of a friend. His eye was lighted up, and his whole countenance beamed voluptuous humour.

Having been early forced into the practice of ſtrict œconomy, he was fully ſenſible of the value of money, and acquired a habit of rejecting all expence which was not abſolutely neceſſary, and the criterion was not his *income*, but his *wants*. With this attention the wages of his labour naturally accumulated, and conſidering him as knowing ſo well how to profit by his talents, he was

T 2

a ſingular

singular instance of prudence being united with genius.

I think if he had lived as long as Mr. Garrick, he would have been at least as rich.

The letters and poems which follow, having no immediate connexion with the anecdotes, it was thought best to insert them at the latter end of the volume. Those letters which are without dates, I have, near as my recollection enabled me, placed in the same progression of time in which they were written.

To

To the Rev. Mr. P———.

London, October 1st, 1769.

I differ from you.—I believe objects of speculation have more power to charm the soul from a sense of its affliction, than *acts* of real and solid benevolence.

The greatness of mind which impels men to beneficent actions, prevents their dwelling upon them. When a man has acquired an habitual generosity, and greatness of soul, the exercise of that generosity, makes little or no durable impression upon his mind; it is become a part of his nature, and performed without attention. It is not so with that species of wisdom which impels the soul to dart into the regions of enquiry and investigation. The spirits are agitated, the

T 3   passions

paſſions are engaged, and expand in the pur-
ſuit.—With what extacy does the mind glow
upon every new acquiſition.—How in a fine
frenzy rolling, doth it

> " Glance from heaven to earth,
> " From earth to heaven,
> " And as imagination bodies forth
> " The forms of things unknown,
> " Turns them to ſhape,
> " And gives to airy nothing,
> " A local habitation and a name."

Every faculty is in exertion—pain, ſick-
neſs, poverty, and all its conſequential
horrors, where are ye—ſunk, loſt, and trembling, at the throne of Genius.—What
but its wondrous potency could invigorate
ſo many great men, and turn the darkneſs
of their dungeon into light.

Hath

Hath not the foul continued its purfuits, with lank and flefhlefs famine on one fide, and reftlefs juftice, bearing in her hand an iron key, on the other. Gracious heaven! When affliction reareth the maffy club! When oppreffion fhaketh the whip of fcorpions!—give me but one fpark of this divine enthufiafm, and I will endure the blow. * * * * * * * * *
* * * * * * * * * * *.

To

To the Rev. Mr. P————.

London, December 21, 1769.

I HAVE received your prefent; I gave one of the pheafants to Mr. ———— I thank you for the other—I ate it where you were *cordially* drank to—make a pun of that, and you may fuppofe we toafted you in Geneva.

I have a defign in meditation, which if it fucceeds I fhall with promptitude convey to you. I reafon upon your temper from my own, and ftate you to myfelf as interefted in all my concerns.———Holland the comedian is dead, and ranting is no more.— Junius is outrageous, but vain is eloquence —obftinancy lofes all fenfes, but that of feeling.—

feeling.—I write this in poor ſpirits and worſe health, an impertinent cold has fixed upon my throat, and a troubleſome pain upon my head, and this I owe to Garrick's playing Haſtings the other night.—I ſhould be tempted to moralize here upon the conſtant ſucceſſion of pain to entertainment, but that I will not uſurp your province.

I long to tranſlate a ſermon of Flechier's *upon Chriſtmas-day*; I never met with an introduction ſo ſuitably majeſtic, and language ſo full of dignity—you may poſſibly have it done by the next year, though I don't know whether it would ſuit your audience.—There is another alſo, upon *the wiſe mens offerings*, which my heart burns to copy.—I never before conſidered their offerings of gold, and myrrh, as emblematical, but only as preſents of honour and humility.

Mr.

Mr. D——— defires to be remembered to you; I gave him a hint of the thirty fermons you received. He looked a little difconcerted, and I believe repents his refufal. ———We have a new comedy; I have not feen it played, but I borrowed the pamphlet, and I do not recollect ever to have read any thing more dull and uninterefting, and yet it fucceeds with the town.

I am, &c.

J. HENDERSON.

To

To Mr. ————.

Who faid, " *He fometimes acted againft the conviction of his feelings, rather than be unlike the reft of the world.*"

London Dec. 25th.

" Dare to be wife,—begin,—for once begun,
" Your tafk is eafy,—half the work is done."

Horace.

A S long as the modes of fafhion continue to be repugnant to wifdom, this
counfel of Horace will deferve the clofeft
attention.   To fteer againft the popular current of error is indeed a noble daring.—A
mere fpeculative theorift, whofe ideas are
gathered, more from the volume of recorded
incidents, than from the fphere they were
acted in, would think it unneceffary to
enjoin

enjoin men to dare to be, that which his books inform him every man ftruggles to be thought; but the man of the world fees inftances every day, either in himfelf or others, where many opportunities of acquiring wifdom, or difplaying it, are neglected, not from actual ignorance, or inaptitude of conception, but from an indolent or cowardly adherence to the reigning fafhions of vice, error, impudence, or prefumption.

True courage encreafes with the profpect of danger. — That there is great danger in oppofing the world in their moft ardent purfuits, every one will allow who has ever felt the bitternefs of neglect, or the poignancy of ridicule.   The foul in almoft every refpect acts fuperior to the body; its fufferings are more acute, its pleafures more exquifite.—Many have by conftitutional vigour dared to expofe their perfons to all the dangers

gers of deftructive war, whofe fpirits are fo
fubject to diftrefs, that popular clamours, or
even the pen of an effayift, can hold them
in the continual perplexities of terror.

This argues a fpecies of courage, very
different from bodily daring to be neceffary
in Horace's advice, and a courage much
fuperior too.

It has fallen within my obfervation, to
fee impertinence and abfurdity, which
fhocked the underftanding of every one
except the fpeaker, by mere dint of re-
folute perfeverance change their forms, and
become, if not admired, at leaft endured.
And indeed it hath been from fuch a confident delivery, that impertinence and error
have forced their way into the world as
they have done. If folly can thus change
opinions, and render itfelf acceptable, how
much

much more fo might wifdom.—I fhall be told, perhaps, that their qualities are fo different as to render the fame modes of perfuafion impracticable.—That error is prefumptuous, and pofitive, and that the concomitants of wifdom, are meeknefs and diffidence.—I do not deny it.—Horace himfelf was of the fame opinion, and therefore recommended it to them by the higheft incitement of honour, to *dare* to be wife. He thought even meeknefs and diffidence virtues that were to be concealed, when the honour of wifdom was in queftion.—You may poffibly quote our great model of chriftianity, as an inftance of wifdom and meeknefs, united in the fame perfon: but I beg leave to obferve, that he never delivered his laws, or his injunctions with timidity—He fuffered for his manly and bold advancement of them. He fuffered with meeknefs, but gave laws with dignity, firmnefs, and vigour.—

The

—The world, I mean the enlightened part of it, have long since received his maxims, and blushed for the dishonour thrown upon the lawgiver.

Horace wrote in times very nearly resembling our own. Folly was popular in Rome, and so was courage; he therefore thought nothing so likely to stimulate his countrymen to wisdom, as an exertion of their favourite passion. He would have, folly vanquished, and lie in chains, to encrease the triumphs of those who added kingdoms to the empire.

Philosophers have been ever accused of want of courage; I think Dryden somewhere calls them, cowards by profession. But in this instance, every one may become a hero. It belongs merely to the soul, and wisdom should be ashamed to nurse any opinion,

nion, which it dare not promulgate and de-
fend.

To shew of how great force example is
among us, I must remark that when a genius
rises, he gives law to thousands; kindles
imaginations that would have otherwise
sunk into torpor, and warms those pens,
which else would have frozen. It would
be the same, my friend, with every other
species of wisdom—Do but dare to begin,
with a resolute purpose and countenance; if
it does not answer, say there is no truth in

SHANDY.

To

To Mr. I———.

From the Banks of the Thames, June 18.

FOR the books you have my beſt thanks. I uſed to think I was fond of fiſhing, but I find it a very dull buſineſs. If the good gentleman of Uz had been devoted to my preſent ſituation, and fixed among ſuch a ſet of aquatic animals, his patience muſt have been exhauſted.* Sir, ſuch a life as I now

* Doctor Franklin's opinion [of angling, may be gueſſed at from the following ſtory, which the ſage often relates to thoſe he thinks *bit* with a taſte for *piſcatory delights*. About ſix o'clock one ſummer morning, (ſaid the philoſopher) as I was riding by the ſide of a running brook in America, I obſerved a gentleman with his fiſhing rod in his hand, a baſket, a bottle, and all the requiſites, by his ſide. I aſked him what ſport?—I have

now lead, is fit for nothing but an otter, and I believe in my confcience the animals I am with are web footed, and have fins. They are neither fifh nor flefh, " *A man knows not where to have them*," but yet I cannot quit thefe *rods,* and *earth worms,* thefe ten days. Think what a treafure was your parcel.

With Mifs Aikin's poems I am delighted, they abound in elegance and fublimity, and in harmony not inferior to

Pope's

not been here more than two hours, was the anfwer.———— When I returned at the clofe of the day, the fame gentle fwain was in exactly the fame place, and at the fame employment. I ftopped my horfe, and afked him if he had been well amufed ? " *Exceeding well,*" was the reply. —Have you caught many fifh ?—" Not any fir."—Had many bites ?———" No, not one bite, but I have had a moft glorious *nibble ! ! !*

Pope's. Indeed, if oppofed to the Effay on Man, *that* verfification is much excelled.

Until the arrival of your's, all the print I could pick up in the houfe, from garret to wine-cellar, was *Bracken's Farriery, Hannah Glaffes Cookery* (which by the way I very much like, for the *laft* receipt in the book is for a *furfeit*) *Pomfret's Poems,* and *Pope's Effay on Man;* which laft I have read through, and think it very inferior to his other ethic epiftles. It is wonderful that a man of fo exquifite a tafte, fo accurate an eye, and fo delicate an ear, fhould have deformed his pages, with fuch abbreviations as *Chanc'lor, Gen'ral, Conqu'rors, Pow'rs, Flow'rs, Ev'ry, Heav'n;* I cannot fee how his lines are fhortened by them. *Heaven* will remain two fyllables in any mode I can pronounce it, let it be fpelled how you will. *Th' eternal, Th' apparent, T' inclofe,* and

U 2

innumerable

innumerable other examples might be quoted. The *philofophy* of the Effay I will not prefume to meddle with, but the *poetry* is fome of it very unworthy of Mr. Pope. Let us look at the firft page.

> " The latent tracts, the giddy heights explore
> Of all who blindly creep, or *fightlefs* foar,
> Eye nature's walks, fhoot folly as it flies,
> And catch the *manners living* as they rife."

Where a word ends with an *S*, a reader finds it unpleafant and difficult to begin the word following with the fame ferpentine letter. Would not *blindly foar*, have been equally poetical, and a better antithefis, than *fightlefs foar*. I fhould think *living manners* would have been quite as clear as *manners living.*—But this would be deemed high treafon in the court of Parnaffus, fo " farewel it," till we meet.

The

The tranflations I have returned by the coach. I made feveral attempts to read them, but all in vain. I could not for the foul of me get thro' three pages. That you may not reproach me with returning the books without an opinion, take the following four lines. I fcribbled them in the marginal leaf of the firft volume, but re-collecting myfelf, thought it would be more modeft*er* to tear out the leaf, than let them remain in the front of the book, in my hand writing.

In holy church we fee divines tranflated,
And mitres oft' times grace the *empty pated.*
How hard, how very hard's an author's fate,
When *empty pated* fellows will tranflate.

If you could get hold of Pontoppidan's Norway, or Pierre Vaude, or Philip Quarles, (I don't mean the Emblem merchant) I

would

would thank you ; though we are likely to do fomewhat better now, for a good pleafant fellow joined our *partie* this morning. I walked with him into the church-yard, but there was nothing worth the trouble of an Epitaph hunter.—He has given me one though which pleafes me.   There is a good climax in it.   Have you ever feen it ?

Dr. Greenwood, his Epitaph on his Wife.

Ah Death ! Ah Death ! thou haft cut down,
The faireft *Green wood* in all .this town ;
Her virtues and her good qualities are fuch,
She was worthy to marry a lord or a judge,
Yet fuch was her condefcenfion, and fuch her hu-
mility,
She chofe to marry me, a Doctor in divinity.
For this heroic deed fhe ftands confeft,
Above all others the phœnix of her fex ;
And like that bird one young fhe did beget,
That fhe might not leave her fex difconfolate.
My grief for her lofs is fo very fore,
I can only write two lines more,

For

For this, and every other good woman's fake,
Never let a blifter be put on a lying-in woman's
back.

This is a ftrange patched letter, part
profe, part verfe, and part neither. But
whatever my letters are, believe that *I* am
with the moft profaic fincerity.

Your's,

J. HENDERSON.

To

To Mr. I———.

Bath, Nov. 2, 1774.

AND fo you have been in France. Prithee Jack tell me, is there that difference in the faces, habits, and characteis, of thefe people, which *appeareth in the lively pour-traitures we fee exhibited of them*; are their women either fo beautiful, or fo engaging as ours. I have not any great ambition to become either dominican, or capuchine, except that I might in either of thofe characters fee a nun *en defhabille*.

I fancy my face would be deemed too *friar-like* already, to be admitted as a *lay-brother*, but that thin, fafting, formal face of thine, would be pofitively a letter of re-commendation, and I think, my friend, you

would

would give an attentive ear to the confeſſions of the young *devotees*, and, upon proper terms, grant them abſolution. I wiſh I had been with you. I long to look at a noviciate;—but for a lady abbeſs—your deſcription hath ſatisfied me.

What you ſay of the French officers agrees with all I have ever heard. They are gentlemen by birth and education. The ſuperior carriage of the ſoldiers is owing to their being ſo univerſally taught fencing, an accompliſhment ſo uſeful, ſo neceſſary, but in this country ſo much neglected. As tactics have never been my ſtudy, I do not feel any great deſire to view their fortifications, notwithſtanding the great things you ſay of them. Marlborough was certainly a fine fellow, and reward was proportioned to his merit; but had even *he* planted twice the number of cannon he had

in

in France, againſt his own Blenheim, and employed *Monſieur Vauban* for his engineer, it would have ſtood the ſhock : ſo maſſy and ponderous is that huge heap of littleneſs, that I believe it will outlaſt the pyramids.

Can their churches exceed Weſtminſter Abbey ?—Thoſe

> " Storied windows, richly dight,
> " Caſting a dim, religious light."

impreſs me with a kind of awe I do not feel in any other place. If I were an abſolute monarch, I would oblige ſuch of my ſubjects as had a fancy for erecting churches, to build them of the Gothic order.

'Tis ſtrange there ſhould be only one good picture at St. Omer's ; but 'tis made up by plenty of *reliques*. I wiſh his Moſt Chriſtian Majeſty were viſited by a dream of heaven and

and Mortimer—But when Salvator's Witch of Endor gives place to a Chinefe painting, and that in the palace he inhabits!—what can we expect?

You fay *Louis Quatorze* will never be forgotten, though he had left no other memorial than the roads, planted and terminated as they are; yet, to an Englifhman, after ten of their *poftes royales*, the profpect moft devoutly to be wifhed is a good fupper, which, it feems, you lacked. But though both H——s and you naufeated frogs, I dare fay you relifhed Burgundy. Yet the juice of the grape, without fome folids, would fhrink a Falftaff to a Mafter Slender. After all, a capon and a cup of fack, are better than fnails and Champagne. Such meagre fare and cold potations——" I hate it,"

I am

· I am now going to dine with a Jew : *his* will be a *Mofaic* treat. Fifn, with oil inftead of fauce, and a turkey ftuffed with garlick was our laft feaft. *This* may, perhaps, be a boiled goofe and peafe-pudding, a ftew of venifon in four cyder, and a mutton-faufage pafty. I wifh the worthies of old would have confidered, before they made fo many laws about eating, that though the tables of the law were very properly in their depart-ments, the dining tables *feemed* more peculiarly in the province of the ladies. If prohibiting what is good be a fin, which I firmly believe it is, both Mofes and Pythagoras have much to anfwer for. They banifhed beans and bacon between them, and that, let me tell you, is no bad difh when a man is hungry, . in fpite of *their philofophy.*

I fuppofe the women are returned, heavy laden with the labours of the loom and the

fpoils

fpoils of the nunnery, and, I hope, efcaped the Cuftom-houfe infpectors.   Farewel: if you, or your *cara fpofa*, will return me as much, and as complete nonfenfe as I have written, I will acknowledge that you have not travelled in vain, nor furveyed ftrange countries for nought.

Your's, ever,

J. H.

To

To Mr. I————.

Bath, October 10*th.*

I BEG your excuse for my silence, but I have such a multitude of business upon my mind, that it takes away my power, and abates much of my inclination to write.

You must not be offended at this, because it contains no disrespect or abatement of the sincere and just affection I have for you.—Make my compliments and thanks to Mrs. ———— for the waistcoat, which is ten times more admired than I am, and the girls will run the length of the parade, to see my flower'd and gilt belly, who would not quit their own threshold to see me. Foote is down here, and I have talked to

him

him a good deal, and dined at a gentleman's where he was, Garrick wrote a letter to Mr. Taylor the other day, which I
faw, and he fpeaks very handfomely of me.
——I play away here in the old way; I
played one new character laft week, (Pierre)
and am preparing with all my might and
main for twelve more at leaft. Doctor
Dodd is here, and I have dined with him
too. Defire Mrs. ——— to believe I love
her, and to leave off abufing me as fhe ufed
to do, and do you think me unalterably,

Your's,

J. HENDERSON.

To

To Mr. I————

Bath, 2d May.

THANKS, thanks, thanks for your care about my mother—you make me very eafy by telling me you intereft yourfelf for her——I cannot write long letters nor good ones now, fo you muft. be content with friendly ones.

It is now one of the firft wifhes of my heart that *————* may fwing, for who-ever injures my dear friend *————* fhall have all the bitternefs of my foul attend him.—Why or wherefore is no matter.—— If I had intereft with the devil, (which by the bye I believe I never fhall have) I would beg a double portion of remorfe and internal torment for that rafcal.

To

To Mr. I———. .

Birmingham, July 8, 1776.

My Dear I——,

IT is very ſtrange to me, that my mother ſhould not have received my letters. I wrote to her the day before I ſet out for this place. I told her of my deſign to paſs my ſummer here—However, on the receipt of your's, I have again written to her. If that letter alſo ſhould miſcarry, pray, my dear friend, tell her that it invited her to live with me at Bath. It told her, that I would procure her an apartment in the ſame houſe with me if I could; if not, I will provide her with a lodging near me; but I rather think and hope, that we may live together. I ſhall be there the latter end of September. There is nothing in my power which I

would

X

would not do, to make that excellent woman happy—She and you Jack, have but one fault, and that is, too great a partiality for a very filly fellow—But be that as it may, I shall be uneasy 'till I have her with me. As to yourself, my worthy friend, I scarce know what to say; my heart longs to talk with you, but its sensations are so simple, and so boyish, I know not how to write them. I love your peace, your happiness, and would I could promote it: I love *——* too; pray tell her so: tell her that no one on earth, except thyself, my friend, can have a better sense of her deserving, or a truer affection for her.

Adieu,

J. HENDERSON.

To Mr. I———.

Birmingham, July 26, 1776.

Dear I———,

I HAVE received a letter from my mother, which I have really had no time to answer, and now I know not where she is. Perhaps you do, for she tells me she should go to London. She objects to coming to Bath, on account of the weight of her baggage, and the expence of its carriage; but that is nothing. Pray tell her, Jack, that I shall be two seasons more at Bath, by articles, and I had rather have her with me, than that she should be liable to inconveniences elsewhere. I find that she has been very ill treated in the country, and my heart aches to think of it; for if there ever was unaffected and genuine simplicity,

 and

and innocence of heart, it is in my mother. I shall not be at ease if I have her not with me; for I not only feel a sense of duty, but a lively and tender affection for her—I know her peculiarities, and can indulge them better than any other person, and I think it will give her happiness to see and know my manner of living, &c. Do, my dearest friend, tell her what I say, and if she wants money let her have it, and I will send you a draft for it without delay.

Believe me,

Your's, &c.

J. H.

To

To Mr. I———.

Birmingham, Aug. 31, 1776.

DEAR I———,

I HAVE had letters from my mother, who will be with me at Bath—She will go through London, and if she calls on you, which I desired her to do, I know your friendship will supply her with any money she may want, and I will remit it to you.

Mrs. Yates is here at present, and we played *The Wonder* last night. You cannot imagine how I am carreſſed by all ranks of people. I shall leave this place covered with Birmingham laurels.

I play with Mrs. Yates again on Monday, *The Roman Father*, and moſt probably

Shylock

Shylock afterwards. Things are ripening for me; I am not forry, even now, that I did not come to London. The end will fhow I fhall do very well—I am, in the mean time, as happy as I have any notion of being. I wifh we could have a day or two together; but for that we muft wait,

Farewell,

J. HENDERSON,

To Mr. I———,

Bath, October 12, 1776,

* * * * * * * * * * * * * * *

* * *.   I am very ill at this writing, and
have been so this week ; but it will go
away, or Doctor Schomberg and I, with a
reinforcement of apothecaries, will drive it
away—I hope you and *———* are in
health ; there is no one's health dearer
to me,

Did I tell you that I have got my mother
here, and am combating with her legion of
gloomy blue D——s too ; but I ought to
do it, and that is enough for me,

Adieu,

X 4   J. H.

To the Reverend Mr. D——

Bath, Feb. 17th, 1776,

Dear Doctor,

I SCARCE know how to begin a
letter, I long to write to you; I have many
times been about to addrefs you, and though
I never wanted, nor ever fhall want a fubject, if I were to write all that my heart
feels towards you; yet after a certain time
has elapfed in filence, one knows not how
to refume the fame familiarity, and with the
fame fpirit, as if no chafm had been made in
our correfpondence; at leaft I feel it fo,——
I fhould hardly have had courage now if
Mr. ———— had not told me you thought
it unkind in me to be filent——I would do
almoft any thing to remove fuch an opinion
from

from your mind, for I love and honour you with sincere attachment, and respect. " Something too much of this."

I shall not wonder if you join with all my friends in town, to condemn my staying here in preference to being in London, because I hear the business has been very partially explained, but I think if it were fairly and fully disclosed to you, I should rather have your approbation. I am naturally timorous, and have an instinctive reluctance to engage in bustle, contention, and intrigue. I have no talents for them, and therefore think it would not be prudent to quit the moderate and quiet path I am in, for such hazardous pursuits. I will tell you, my most dear friend, the simple principle on which I acted, and I think it almost an *axiom*. If I am really wanted on the London stage, I ought to be placed there

on

on honourable and advantageous terms, and
I fhould be fo. If I am *not* really wanted,
I have no bufinefs there, nor can the defign of having me there be other than treacherous and pernicious. Yet farther. It
was only propofed to engage me for one
year; a propofal by which the manager
hazarded nothing, as the very novelty of
one who had been talked of as I had been,
would have paid in very few nights the falary I was to receive; and *I* hazarded *every
thing by it.*

My friend W———* tells me he has
thoughts of taking orders, a view which
I am perfuaded you will encourage, and
promote, as he certainly has not, any
more than myfelf, talents for bufinefs and
chicane; I was very fenfibly touched with
his misfortunes, and think the church is
the only afylum he can meet with from
them,

them. But you will judge better than I can.

I hope, my dear friend, you have health, and that is all I need wish to such a heart, and such a capacity as yours; felicity and honour will naturally follow such goodness, and such understanding, if their operations are not retarded by sickness.

Believe me, &c.

J. HENDERSON.

Infcribed under the Picture of a Lady who had flighted the Author.

(Written in 1769.)

ONWARD it preffes with an eager view,
More fplendid fcenes, and tranfports to purfue;
Far as ambition's piercing eye can fee,
Nor once regards humility and me.
No gentle blandifhments arreft its fpeed,
Nor once it ftops, though love and meeknefs bleed,
Bleed in its path, and tremble in its courfe,
Weak ties have love, againft ambition's force.

By pleafure urg'd—urg'd by ambition's fting,
From love, from me, from tendernefs you fpring,
Your picture, faithful to your heart as face,
Eludes my grafp, and mocks my fond embrace,
No more from folemn thought to mirth I fly,
No more the heart exults, no more the eye
Darting abroad, collects each fcattered ray,
Which humour beam'd, and fancy led aftray.

Infcribed

*Inscribed under a Print of Orpheus playing
ou his Lyre, being the Frontispiece to a
young Lady's Music Book.*

(Written in 1768.)

WHEN Orpheus sung, or sweetly touch'd his lyre,
Such heav'n born sounds the woods and groves inspire;
The rugged rocks, and wood-clad mountains dance,
And wild with pleasure, at his song advance;
Such melody stern Pluto's soul disarms,
From Pluto's throne Eurydice it charms.
At length by cruel hands bereav'd of breath,
(For music's self cannot contend with death)
The shepherds all their rural sports forsook,
And every eye assum'd a mournful look,
Each nymph felt anguish—grief felt ev'ry swain,
In place of harmony, see discord reign.
Long in this state men liv'd, and had remain'd
So now——But you, my fair, have deign'd
To sooth our cares, and soften all our grief,
And brought sweet melody to our relief.

So

So foft the founds, of grace and eafe poffeft;
Such airs melifluous humanize each breaft,
No longer need you envy Orpheus' fame,
Since a new Orpheus reigns in *————'s name.

A Receipt to make a Paftoral.

TAKE firft two handfuls of wild thyme,
Or any herb that fuits your rhyme,
And fhred it finely o'er your plains,
Fit to receive your rolling fwains.
With crocus, violets, and daifies,
Be fure to fill the vacant places;
Then plant your groves and myrtle bowers,
(Well water'd with celeftial fhowers)
And, to avoid the critics quarrel,
A fprig or two of Virgil's laurel.
Your ground thus laid, your trees thus plac'd,
Sweeten'd with flow'rs to your tafte,
Your fhepherd take, and as is wont,
Baptize him at the poet's font.
Adorn him with fcrip, crook, and reed,
And lay him by for farther need.

Then

Then take a damfel neat and fair,

And in a fillet bind her hair,

Give her a flock of tender fheep,

And keep her by you—She will keep.

An Imitation of a French Paſtoral:

I

DAPHNIS one day his flock had led
    Into a verdant grove :
Not far off, Phillis in the fhade,
    Had brought her lambs to rove :
Both of them met each other,
       Her Daphnis faw,
       Him Phillis faw,
Each of them faw the other.

II.

Good day, fweet fheepherdefs, faid he,
    Shepherd faid fhe good day,
In yonder orchard prithee fee,
    The grafs how frefh and gay ;

Both inftantly went thither ;
  Daphnis fat down,
  Phillis fat down,
They both fat down together.

III.

A nofegay then of violets made,
 For Phillis the fhepherd pull'd,
Phillis for him, in order laid
 Some flowers nicely cull'd,
Both offer'd them each other ;
  Her's, Daphnis took,
  His, Phillis took,
Each took them of the other.

IV.

Permit, upon thy breaft, he cry'd,
 That I this nofegay place,
With mine the pretty lafs replied,
 I'd fain thy bofom grace.
Both granted one another ;
  His, Daphnis plac'd,
  Her's, Phillis plac'd,
Fach plac'd them on the other.

V. To

V.

To ever true and conſtant be,
   Make me, ſaid he, a vow,
To conſtant be, and true, ſaid ſhe,
   The ſame to me do thou;
Both promis'd one another.
     This Daphnis did,
     This Phillis did,
They did ſo by each other.

The following little Fragment he wrote soon after his arrival at Bath. There is, I think, a sort of whimsical humour about it, somewhat resembling the *Historie* which Mr. Henderson read into reputation: but as neither John Gilpin's Race, nor Mr. Henderson's very *outré* manner of reading it, ever gave me any very extatic pleasure, I think some apology necessary to the reader, for inserting an imperfect Ballad.

A New Ballad.

YE lords and lordlings lend an ear,
  No wicked lies I write,
The truth most truly you shall hear,
  For your eafe and delight.

In Bath a wine-merchant did dwell,
  And C——y was his name,
Who by the blessing of the muse,
  I now transmit to fame.

This

This wine-merchant a daughter had,
  A daughter brown had he,
Who when fhe wore both cap and fhoes,
  Reach'd to her father's knee.

When other miffes dreft their dolls,
  She dreft her mind, I ween,
And when her play-mates made dirt pies,
  She at her book was feen.

Full broad the ribband which fhe wore,
  To bind her head around,
And right fantaftic were the fhoes,
  Which kept her from the ground.

And now, when time had form'd her ear,
  To mufic fhe it bent,
And pleas'd the neighboring gentles all,
  And all folks where fhe went.

Her father grew exceeding proud,
  Exceeding proud grew he,
And afk'd the gentles all around,
  His daughter for to fee.

Hoping

Hoping, that fome of noble birth,
　　Would be caught by a fong,
And carelefs of her low eftate,
　　In wedlock bind her ftrong.

The gentles ftar'd, and knew not what
　　To do, or what to fay;
They wip'd their faces as they could,
　　They bow'd, and came away.

Now fee how pride deftroyeth all
　　The knowledge God hath fent,
Sith he who ferv'd full many a man,
　　Could harbour fuch intent.

For once, before his heart grew proud,
　　A livery he wore,
And us'd to wait with hat in hand,
　　His mafter to the door.

So well he did in this behave,
　　So humble then did feem,
That no one thought of pride or ftate,
　　This merchant e'er could dream.

The

The nobles, therefore, notic'd him,
   And bought his wine, to ſhew
That merit they would patronize,
   Though ſprung from ne'er ſo low.

Yet all this while no lordling came,
   With offer of his hand,
Nor ſquireling ſpruce, nor parſon trim,
   With caſſock and with band.

What ſhall I do, the father cry'd,
   My daughter will grow old,
And all her wit, and all her voice,
   Will ſerve her but to ſcold.

Then to the ſynagogue went he,
   And brought out many a Jew,
To hear her play, and hear her ſing,
   And of her take a view.

From Pontus, and from Phrygia,
   From Cappadocia eke,
Theſe wandering pilgrims came I ween,
   Two or three times a week.

Y 3

They

They fat, they heard, and took their fnuff,
　And wondering, roll'd their eyes,
And then protefted,—that without
　Some wine they could not rife.

Then Franco thin, and Cappa fat,
　Declar'd upon their word,
They thought her for a Jew too good,
　And bid her wed a lord.

But now comes on a dreadful tale,
　I tremble to relate,
Oh, that fome lord, or bifhop had,
　Torn out this leaf of fate.

To Bath there came a ftrange young man,
　Nobody knew from whence ;
Prefuming on fome foolifh gifts,
　Of talent and of fenfe.

Unto the playhoufe ftraight he went,
　The manager to fee,
Who gave immediately confent,
　A player he fhould be.

The

The day was fixt, the day was come,
   That he fhould firft appear,
When lo. in Hamlet as he ftood,
   He fhook his hat with fear.

This damfel faw, this damfel figh'd,
   And bath'd her jetty eyes,
And faid, my heart is near breaking,
   For Hamlet when he dies,

The father ftorm'd, and lock'd his doors,
   This player to prevent,
Swore, like Ophelia, fhe fhould drown,
   Before he'd give confent.

But fay what bolts or bars, can keep
   A woman from her will;
'Tis more than mortal man can do,
   * * * * * * * * * *.

Cætera defunt.

E P I G R A M

On Artaxerxes, and other Operas, performed at the Theatres.

OUR Engliſh ſtage, which was at firſt deſign'd,
To raiſe the genius, and improve the mind,
To expoſe the various follies of the town;
Seems *now* contented to expoſe *its own*.

The Blighted Wreath.

VIVID and green, the laurel Roſcius wore,
Still water'd with the foſtering dew of praiſe,
  'Till vanity and avarice ſwore,
To have a pluck at his long-envied bays.

  They waited on him—welcome gueſts they were,
And artful, took poſſeſſion of his heart;
  Then ſtrove to blaſt, the wreath they could not tear,
With venom foul, infus'd by ſpecious art.

Moſt

Moſt natural magic, and dire property,
Alas, too plainly to the world were ſeen,
On wholeſome fame uſurp'd immediately,
And ſickly yellow gain'd upon the green.

Almoſt, each night, ſome leaf its verdure loſt,
Yet they his weak and cred'lous heart conſol'd ;
They bade him prize his laurel by its coſt,
When ev'ry leaf ſhould be transform'd to gold.

Pernicious alchemy ! ah, treacherous friends,
How could you, nature's darling thus deceive ;
That you have compaſs'd your inſidious ends,
The ſoul of Shakeſpeare, and the muſe ſhall grieve.

Ah, what avails it, that on Thames's ſhore,
Three hundred thouſand pounds his banker keeps,
Whilſt Phœbus and the Muſes all deplore,
His avarice waking, whilſt his genius ſleeps.

Theſe pounds, indeed, will many a flatterer buy ;
But ah ! where then are brother George's hopes ;
Theſe pounds, were doom'd his children to ſupply,
Not pay for ſcribbling *metaphors* and *tropes*.

An

An Impromptu on Mr. GARRICK's Funeral.

AS from the borders of Cocytus' wave,
Not yet enfranchis'd by the clofing grave,
Garrick juft peep'd into the world above,
And faw a fombrous long proceffion move;
Saw the ftrand glitter with the tawdry ftate,
Part grave, part gay, part tinfel, and part plate;
The prim deportment of lugubrious mutes,
And the taught toffings of the feather'd brutes.

" Another jubilee, he cried, appears,
" Go bid the managers difmifs their fears;
" No more from empty theatres defpair,
" And dread of duns, deliver to the air !
" Call all my carpenters—bid George attend,
" And ranfack Monmouth-ftreet from end to end;
" Buy all the blacks, defraud the ftarving moth,
" Or let him, if he will, defile the cloth:
" Bring moth and all—we have no time to lofe—
" If there's not black enough, then buy the blues.

" Dye

" Dye all the truncheons, and their edges gild,
" All but that truncheon I was wont to wield;
" Buy from the paſtry-cooks their twelfth-night flags,
" To flame in front, the rear be cloth'd with rags;
" The dirtieſt wardrobe will the rear ſupply,
" Our ſtage perſpective will deceive the eye:
" All to your ſeveral offices repair,
" Whilſt I determine—in what place or where,
" This gaudy mummery may beſt appear.
" If for Ophelia, by young Hamlet mourn'd;
" Or for poor Juliet, yet alive inurn'd."

Thus far he ſpoke, in an imperial tone,
And quite forgot the funeral was his own.

Alas, poor Garrick, in Elyſian meads,
Where new delight to new delight ſucceeds;
Still ſhall the phantom wealth thy ſteps purſue,
And tinge thy pleaſures with a *careful* hue.

The two foregoing Jeu d'Eſprits I ſeveral
years ago ſubmitted to the inſpection of my
friend, Mr. Mickle, whoſe tranſlation of

the

the Lufiad will remain a monument of his poetic talents, while this country retains tafte for luxuriant imagery, adorned with harmonius numbers—He thought that they contained much wit, but more feverity, and hoped that Mr. Garrick's various powers as an actor, and generofity as a friend, would be held in remembrance, when his little foibles, as a man, were forgotten; and that it was rather unfair to lafh *his* memory for the gaudy mummery of a funeral, originating in the folly and ridiculous vanity of furviving friends. " I will fhow you (faid he) what is my opinion of Mr. Garrick," and gave me the following lines.

Upon *Mr.* G A R R I C K.

By Mr. M I C K L E.

FAIR was the graceful form Prometheus made,
Its front, the image of the God difplayed:
All heaven approved it, e'er Minerva ftole
The fire of Jove, and kindled up the foul.

So Shakefpeare's page, the flower of poefy,
E'er Garrick rofe, had charms for every eye;
'Twas nature's genuine image, wild and grand,
The ftrong marked picture of a mafter's hand.

But when *his* Garrick—Shakefpeare's Pallas came,
The Bard's bold painting burft into a flame:
Each part, new force and vital warmth received,
As touched by heaven—and all the picture lived.

ERRATA.

Page.	Line.		
15	2	*read* circumſtances——*for* circumſtance.
22	3	thy	thine.
42	8	he	it.
45	7, and 8——ſhould not be divided, but the ſame paragraph continued.		
91	12	*read* hands————*for* ſtands.
105	18	witches	wiſhes.
125	3	wit	wits.
138	2	Dec. 22, 1774	Oct. 24, 1772.
196	7	manner in which he——manner he.
196	8	juſtified	ſatisfied.
218	2	1778	1780.
224	4	unwillingly	unwilling.
290	11	are not inferior	not inferior.
294	12	were	are.